Identity Crisis

4th revised edition

Also by Debbi Mack

Sam McRae Novels

Least Wanted

Riptide

Deep Six

Other Novels

Invisible Me

The Planck Factor

Short Stories

Five Uneasy Pieces

Identity Crisis

A Sam McRae Mystery

Debbi Mack

Renegade Press
Savage, MD

Renegade Press
P.O. Box 156
Savage, MD

Library of Congress Cataloging-in-Publication Data
Identity Crisis; 4th rev. ed.
ISBN: 978-0-9906985-8-6
Library of Congress Control Number: 2017962343

Dedication

This book is dedicated to my husband, Rick Iacangelo, who provided the unconditional support and encouragement that helped make it a reality.

This book is also dedicated to my father and fellow writer, Frank Andrew Mack, who never got to see the book but always believed in me.

Chapter ONE

I've never been a morning person, and if there's one thing I don't need before my first cup of coffee, it's a visit from the cops. But at 8:45 on a Friday morning, two of them waited for me at my law office.

I shut the door on the steam heat—typical July weather in Maryland—and shook my sticky blouse loose. Seven years in practice had taught me many hard lessons. One of them should have been never to wear dry-clean-only blouses in the summer.

Sheila, the seventy-plus receptionist and secretary for the accounting firm where I sublet space, gave me a brief wave while answering the phone through her ever-present headset. Her long, bony fingers clacked away at the keyboard without skipping a beat.

Both men stood as I approached. I recognized Detective Martin Derry of the Prince George's County police. I wondered what the homicide investigator wanted with me.

"Good morning," I said.

"Morning, Ms. McRae." Derry had light blue eyes, the color of lake water in January. "I need to speak to you about one of your clients."

Derry's companion was tall and gangly, as if loosely constructed of mismatched bones. His frizzy reddish-blonde hair was short, making his head seem too small and his nose and ears too big. He peered at me with his head cocked to one side, like a pigeon.

"Let me have five minutes, OK?"

Derry nodded, and I trudged up the steps to my office. I didn't have any clients charged with homicide. Since I'd left the public defender's office, most of my criminal clients were yuppies with first-time DWIs or habitual traffic offenders, so I was dying to find out what he wanted. Whatever it was, it could wait five more minutes.

I went through the daily routine of opening the Venetian blinds, turning down the thermostat on the ancient window unit, and booting my computer. I started a pot of dark roast coffee, placing my mug on the burner to catch it as it dripped out. When I felt ready, I invited them in.

They each did a cop's visual sweep of my office before they sat down. No doubt, they were impressed by the plush furnishings—a used desk, two guest chairs, a metal filing cabinet, a small hutch for my supplies, and tables for my fax, copier, and Mr. Coffee, most of which I'd bought at a state surplus outlet. My one indulgence was a new high-backed desk chair.

"This is Special Agent Carl Jergins, FBI," Derry said.

"Sam McRae," I said, extending my hand. Jergins worked my arm like a pump. FBI? I wondered what was up.

Derry sat stiffly upright. Dark-haired and mustached, he had a solemn, squarish face. In a charcoal gray suit, starched white shirt, and red tie, Derry was one of those people who manage to look dapper, no matter what. We'd met years before when I'd defended the man accused of killing his fiancée. Derry treated me with complete, almost excessive, professionalism. I tried to ignore the charged feeling in the air when he was around.

"We understand you have a client named Melanie Hayes," Derry said.

I stared at him. "She's not—" I couldn't finish the thought.

"No. It's her ex, Tom Garvey. He was found shot to death."

"Oh, my God."

"We know you represented her in a domestic violence matter," Derry said, watching me closely as he spoke. "You understand why we need to talk to her."

I nodded. "When did this happen?"

"Over the weekend," Derry said.

"I'll be present when you question her." It was not a request.

Derry bobbed his head in brief acknowledgment. "When was the last time you spoke to Ms. Hayes?"

"Last Friday."

"On the phone or in person?"

"In person. She came to the office."

"And you haven't spoken to her since?"

"No. Why?"

Derry leaned back in his chair. He appeared to think about whether to answer the question.

"There's a problem," he said. "She seems to have disappeared."

"What? Just vanished?"

"She hasn't been home and hasn't shown up for work all week."

An angry sizzle interrupted my thoughts. The odor of burnt coffee filled the room. My cup was overflowing onto the hot plate.

"Shit." I jumped up and exchanged the cup for a carafe. Coffee was everywhere. In haste, I ripped a couple of pages from a writing pad and daubed at the mess, grinning sheepishly at the cops.

Derry's mustache twitched into a brief grimace. Jergins stared.

"Well, I have no idea where she could be," I said, swiping at drops that had landed on my blouse.

Both cops studied me, maybe waiting for more. I sat down and drank my coffee. The air conditioner clicked and roared in the background.

Jergins cleared his throat, leaning forward. "Ms. McRae," he said, in a gruff, rat-a-tat voice, "it's extremely important that we get in touch with Ms. Hayes as soon as possible. Her life may be at risk."

"Why? And what's the FBI's interest in this?" I looked directly at the bony fed.

Jergins' nostrils flared as if he'd detected a bad smell. From the look in his beady eyes, you'd have thought I was the source.

"Has your client ever mentioned the name Gregory Knudsen?"

"No. Who is he?"

"What about Christof Stavos?"

"What about him?" I asked, a little annoyed that he'd ignored my question.

"Have you heard that name? Ever?"

"Nope. Never ever."

Jergins did that pigeon move with his head again.

I resisted the urge to imitate him.

He said, "Mr. Stavos is a sick and dangerous man. It's absolutely essential that Ms. Hayes get in touch with us as soon as possible. For her own safety, if nothing else."

"Why?" I asked. "Who is he?"

"Wiseguy from New York."

The phone rang.

I decided to let the voice mail get it. "Mafia? What would someone like that want with my client?"

Jergins leaned back, allowing himself a dramatic pause. "Did your client leave anything with you? A CD, maybe?"

"No."

"And she never mentioned Knudsen?"

"Like I said, no."

He nodded, still not looking satisfied.

"So, who is this guy, Knudsen?" I said. "And what's on the CD?"

Jergins said nothing.

"Let's get back to your client," Derry said. "Did she ever mention anything about leaving town? Even a hint that she might?"

I spread my hands in a helpless gesture. "Not that I recall."

Derry appeared to ponder my response then said, "I guess we've taken enough of your time."

Jergins looked like he wanted to subpoena every piece of paper in the room.

"Wait a second," I said. "What's going on? Obviously, someone's been murdered, but is there more?"

Derry glanced at Jergins, who remained mute.

"There's got to be," I said. "Or why would the FBI be involved?"

Another look passed between the men.

Derry said, "Right now, I'm concerned about investigating a homicide."

As opposed to what? I wanted to ask.

"This mobster—what was his name? Stavos?—he's also a suspect?" I asked.

Silence.

Forget it, I thought. I might as well go outside and ask a fire hydrant.

As they stood up, Derry said, "You'll let us know if you hear from Ms. Hayes."

"Of course."

Jergins pulled out a business card and thrust it toward me. It said he was with the field office in Baltimore.

"You hear anything about Knudsen, you let me know," he said, in his clipped monotone. Probably picked it up watching too many reruns of *Dragnet*.

After they left, I checked my voice mail. Someone named Christy from my credit card company had called. I was up to date on my bill, and the message didn't say anything about their "great new services." Curious, I dialed the number and connected directly with Christy, who sounded like a college student working the phones during her summer break.

"Stephanie Ann McRae?" she said. The credit card was in my full name rather than the acronym I use as a nickname. "I'm calling to confirm your recent application for a line of credit," she continued, sounding as if she were reading from cue cards.

"But I haven't applied for more credit."

A few seconds of silence. "You haven't? Oh, wow. Have you lost your card recently?"

"No, no. I would have reported that." I pulled my purse out of my desk, just to check. The card was still in my wallet.

"Well, it looks like someone has applied for a credit line in your name," Christy said. "I'm glad we were able to catch this. The amount is unusually large."

"How large would that be?"

"Ten thousand dollars."

Chapter TWO

It's one of those things you think will never happen to you," I said. "I still can't believe it. I'm just glad they caught the problem. Do you know how long it would've taken to clear my credit?"

"Mmm-mmm," Jamila murmured, about the best she could manage with a spicy meatball hors d'oeuvre in her mouth.

I had a ginger ale in one hand and a small plate loaded with shrimp and little quiches in the other. This left me with no hands to eat either the shrimp or the quiches. I set my drink on a handy table, hoping that none of the waiters patrolling the banquet room would scoop it up when I wasn't looking.

Close to a hundred people had shown for the mixer, which surprised the hell out of me. The bar association doesn't usually schedule events during the summer. The theory, I guess, is that most people take summer vacations. It was a sad commentary on our profession that we were there.

"So I'm finally checking my credit history," I said. "They say you should do it every year. I've always found a reason to put it off until now. Hopefully, the jerk hasn't applied for ten more credit cards with my information."

"Unbelievable."

"I almost didn't come. I don't want to see any of these people. Present company excepted, of course."

Jamila gestured with her Diet Coke. "Roger's trashed." She referred to the partner she worked for at Haskins & O'Connell, one of the biggest firms in the county.

I looked across the room at Roger. He was smiling, talking amiably to some guy in a nine-hundred-dollar suit, and looking as dull as ever. "How the hell can you tell?"

"Cause he keeps licking his lips." Jamila straightened and did another quick survey of the room. "You see any judges? There are supposed to be some judges at this damn thing."

"I don't know. I just came for the free food."

Jamila smiled and continued to look around. As usual, she was dressed to the nines. Her dusky brown complexion was a perfect complement to her tan suit, and she'd applied her makeup with surgical precision. She aspired to partnership at H&O and, eventually, a judgeship with the Circuit Court for Prince George's County. Maybe even the federal court in Greenbelt.

In P.G. County, a Washington, D.C., suburban area with a majority black population, her appointment to such a position was a distinct possibility if she kept her nose clean and went to the right parties. Jamila had been a good friend of mine since law school, but with any luck, nobody would hold that against her.

"I'm sorry about your problem," she said. "Can you believe, the same thing happened to one of my clients? Only no one caught it, and he's in the hole *twenty* thousand dollars."

"Damn."

"He was supposed to close on some property next month. Now the lender's trying to back out. We're hoping to fix things before the closing date, but you know what our chances are of doing that?"

"Pretty slim."

"We may have to put off the closing," Jamila said. "Or even cancel it. All because of some little shit who … I'm sorry. I don't mean to go on about my problems. We were talking about you."

"It's OK." I reached for my drink, but it had been spirited away. "What gets me is, I'm so careful. I tear up my junk mail. I never give out my social security number to strangers. I rarely buy anything on the Internet. But that's not enough anymore."

Jamila said something about recent criminal laws against identify theft that got drowned out by guffaws.

"Don't you have to find people before you can prosecute them?" I asked, raising my voice above the din.

"That's what I'm saying. We had to hire a private investigator. Reed Duvall. Ever hear of him?"

I shook my head. "Most of my clients can't afford me, let alone a detective."

"He's supposed to be good. A little unconventional, but they say he gets the job done."

"I wonder if he could find my missing client."

"How's that?"

"The police are looking for this woman I represented in a domestic violence hearing. We were going to go back to court to enforce the order. Now, her ex is dead and the police can't find her."

"Oh." She raised an eyebrow.

"Hey, it's innocent until proven guilty, remember?"

"That's what they say."

I filled Jamila in on what the cops told me, leaving Melanie's name out of it.

"The FBI," she said. "Shit."

"The whole thing looks weird as hell, no question. Thing is, I have no duty to do anything. I don't have to find her."

"If she shows up, tell her to go to the cops," Jamila said.

"Sure. But I keep wondering what the Mob has to do with this. And how is my client involved? If I don't act, is she going to end up being another story on the eleven o'clock news?"

Jamila's glance darted toward the door. "Judge Ridgway just came in. We should say hello."

"Goody."

She shot me a look. "You've got to learn to work these people, sweetie."

I sighed. "I know. It's such a friggin' drag."

"And another thing. You can't take responsibility for everything that happens to a client and stay sane in this business."

"Yeah, yeah." I knew it all too well. Still, I was concerned about Melanie. For one thing, I simply couldn't picture her as a killer.

φ φ φ

I don't like domestic violence cases, but for Melanie I made an exception. Maybe it helped that, like me, she was 36 and single. She was tall and slender with brown hair cut in a short bob. Her intelligence and forthrightness impressed me. She had an air of quiet resolve—no hysterics, no second-guessing about whether she was doing the right thing. She had everything you look for in a client—a rational and cooperative attitude plus the ability to pay. Not that the case brought in much money, but it never hurts when a client can pay.

Getting the order hadn't been difficult. Tom had been drunk and abusive. When he'd hit Melanie, there'd been a minor scuffle. She'd called the police, and they'd arrested Tom.

Afterward, he'd moved in with a friend in Laurel. Things were fine for a while, then the phone calls started. He started coming by her apartment.

She refused to talk to him. She hoped he would give up, but he wouldn't.

"I want him to leave me alone," she said, staring out my office window at the brick storefronts of Laurel's historic Main Street. She seemed anxious the last time I saw her. I tried to be reassuring. Unfortunately, getting the orders in these cases is one thing and getting the abusers to comply is something else.

φ φ φ

Later that afternoon, I tried to reach Melanie at home, without success. I didn't have a cell phone number, so I tried First Bank of Laurel, where she worked as an assistant manager. Melanie wasn't there. I asked for Donna Thurman, her boss. I had done some work for Donna before, and she'd given Melanie my name.

Donna came on the line. "Yes?" she said, her vocal chords sounding as taut as piano wires.

"Donna, it's Sam McRae. Do you have a minute to talk?"

"Well …"

She sounded busy, so I got to the point. "Have you seen Melanie lately?"

I thought I heard her gasp at the other end. Maybe it was just the phone line.

"Sam," she said, "I'm … I'm in the middle of something. Can we meet at your office later?"

"Sure."

Around four thirty, Donna came by. Somewhere in her sixties, she was a petite, silver-haired wonder with skin tanned to a carcinogenic brown from frequent sailing trips on the Chesapeake with her husband. Donna was the kind of person who, rather than soften with age, grew more angular. Instead of slowing down, she seemed to be picking up speed, as if her life were a game of *Beat the Clock*.

She wore a short-sleeved yellow suit and, normally, would have looked terrific. However, when she came into the office, I could tell something was wrong. I'd never seen her so subdued and drawn. I wondered if she was sick.

"Thank heavens it's Friday," she said, collapsing into a chair with a muted grunt. "Sam, I'm so worried about Melanie. She hasn't been at work all week. She hasn't called. It's not like her. I even thought about filing a missing person's report. Then the police came."

"I guess you don't have any idea where she might be."

She shook her head.

"When was the last time you saw her?" I asked.

"Last Friday, at work."

"Did you talk to her over the weekend?"

"No."

"It's frustrating, but there's not much we can do at this point. I hope she shows up."

Donna hunched forward, her expression suggesting there was more on her mind. "That FBI agent. He said something about the Mob being involved. The whole thing is so bizarre—and scary. I've been trying to figure how to tell her parents."

"Her parents?"

"I've known them for years. They moved to Arizona a while ago, but I keep in touch with them. I remember when Melanie was born."

"Could Melanie have gone there due to a family emergency?"

"I suppose it's possible," she said, "but Melanie hasn't spoken to her parents in years. Besides, I think I would have heard about it."

"What about brothers and sisters?"

"Melanie's an only child."

I shrugged. "Maybe she decided to take a vacation or something."

"She wouldn't do that without telling us."

"Well, you know her better than I do. I didn't realize you were so close."

"I helped her get this job." Donna looked sheepish. "To be honest, it's a little embarrassing for me at work, what with her disappearing like this."

"I take it Melanie never mentioned any of the stuff the police asked about?"

"Heavens, no."

"Did she ever talk about Tom?"

"Not much, though I could tell they were having problems. You know, how it is. Sometimes, you can just tell. Now and then, she'd mention his drinking and his building debt. Tell you the truth," she said, arching a knowing eyebrow, "I wasn't all that surprised. The better I got to know him, the more I realized he was all surface, all charm."

I let her vent for a bit about Tom. She hadn't approved of his moving in with Melanie, and the fact that it hadn't worked out didn't help matters. I still wasn't sure why she'd wanted to meet me, but Donna was a good client—a friend—so I let her take her time getting to the real reason for her visit.

Donna shifted restlessly. "I'd like to ask a favor."

"Yes?"

"I ran by Melanie's apartment yesterday. Her car was there, but she didn't answer my knock. After what the police said, I started wondering ... what if she couldn't get to the door? What if she was passed out ... or worse?"

I'd also wondered if Melanie might be dead, but I hadn't wanted to bring it up. "I guess we can't rule that out, but don't jump to conclusions. It's possible she wasn't home."

"But what about her car?"

"She could have taken a cab or a bus."

"Maybe she saw me through the peephole and didn't answer the door."

"Why would she do that?"

She hesitated. "Probably ashamed to talk to me. Since things fell apart with Tom ... well, we haven't spoken to each other much." She paused, then asked, "Could you run by her place and check on her? It's not far from here."

I nodded. "Sure. I don't know if I'll have any more luck, but at least I can say I tried."

"I appreciate that, Sam." Donna smiled, looking abashed. "I guess I must seem like a silly old woman. I know she's grown and able to take care of herself. Maybe it's because I never had kids of my own. She's all alone, and I do almost consider her like a daughter."

"Don't worry about it. She's probably fine." I hoped I was right.

φ φ φ

After work, I stopped at my place to feed Oscar, my fifteen-pound, black and white cat, and grabbed something to eat. Dinner was two pieces of toast with peanut butter and salad-in-a-bag. I'm not much of a cook, and it hardly seems worth it to dirty dishes just to feed myself. I finished the meal with chocolate chip cookie dough ice cream straight from the carton. I rinsed the silverware and the plate and headed for Melanie's place.

My '67 Mustang sputtered on the first turn of the ignition key and the second, then finally roared to life. It was an old relic, painted a Welch's grape purple and in need of a tune-up and a patch job on the muffler, which made noises that attracted curious glances from five hundred yards. It could probably have used a trip through the car wash, too. But it ran—noise, dirt, and all.

Melanie lived in the Whiskey Bottom neighborhood of North Laurel, a collection of *très* suburban brick townhouses and apartments just across the county line. Maybe there'd been a lot of moonshining in that area at one time because the booze theme could be found on most of the street signs, which had names like Moonshine Hollow, Bourbon Street, Brandy Lane, and Barrelhouse Road.

I found a space near the attractive three-story apartment building swathed in greenery and accented with beds of bright red begonias. Donna said Melanie had a red Geo with a crystal hanging from the rearview mirror. It was still there. The heat of the day radiated from the blacktop as I crossed the lot. The air was heavy with humidity, but four young teens—two girls and two boys—were outside, engaged in a bit of friendly competition, shooting hoops at a freestanding basket. Watching them made me sweat.

Melanie had mail in her box. Not a lot, but maybe a couple of days' worth. The building had an open foyer, and her apartment was one of four located on the second floor.

I climbed the steps. No newspaper lay on the mat before her door. I heard a TV set, but couldn't tell from where. I knocked and waited, then knocked again. No one answered.

Just for kicks, I checked under the mat for a spare key and found one. What a lousy place for it. There aren't many options for apartment dwellers, but I wouldn't put my key under the mat.

I picked it up, feeling a little odd about walking into someone's apartment uninvited. But Melanie would thank me later if she was in there, dying on the floor. I used the key in the deadbolt, which unlocked with no problem. It also fit the knob. Turning it, I stepped inside.

The door opened into a combined living room/dining area. Closed curtains made the place gloomy. Even so, I could see a chair turned onto its side and things strewn over the floor. Someone had ransacked the place.

Chapter THREE

I stood at the door, looking and listening. The neighbor's television continued to buzz in the background, but I didn't hear anything else. Finally, I took a few tentative steps inside.

At first, I thought it was the work of vandals. Her stereo and VCR lay on the floor, the housing on each ripped off. Same for the TV set.

At the same time, everything looked too neat. The stuff on the floor wasn't thrown about, but arranged in piles. A few videos here, books there—as if someone had cleared everything off to dust, then didn't bother to put it back.

I wondered if the cops could have done this. Assuming they'd gotten a search warrant, this seemed like overkill for them. Then I saw her CD collection.

Someone had opened all the jewel cases and tossed them aside in a heap. I thought about what Agent Jergins said about Christof Stavos looking for a CD. The thought that the Mob could have been there made my stomach clench.

I did a quick survey of the apartment. Every room was much the same. Dishes, pots, and pans were stacked on any available surface in the kitchen. The dressers and closet in the bedroom had been emptied, their contents heaped on the floor.

Thankfully, I didn't find Melanie dead or disabled. Of course, that wasn't proof positive that she wasn't.

I checked each room again, more methodically this time, looking for something like a travel brochure, a credit card receipt, anything. In the kitchen, I picked through some stuff that looked like it came from a "junk" drawer—take-out menus, scissors, a bar napkin, rubber bands, and a small ball of string.

I took a closer look at the napkin. It was from Aces High, a strip joint a few miles up Route 1. The logo was an Ace of Spades with a half-naked woman, eyes closed and lips parted in the throes of ecstasy, sprawled across it. Someone had written "Connie" and a phone number on it. A friend of Tom's, I supposed. Apparently, drinking and debt weren't his only vices. I wrote the name and number in a small notebook I carry.

The bathroom didn't offer much. The bedroom was a mess. I decided to assume for the sake of not taking all night that what I was looking for wasn't in her clothing. Chances were it was on her dresser or in the wastepaper basket. I checked both and came up empty.

A small, dark blue address book, with an envelope tucked inside like a bookmark, lay on the bedside table next to the phone. The envelope was unsealed. Inside was a receipt for a post office box and a key. The stamp indicated a College Park zip code. According to the paper, the renter was Stephanie A. McRae.

I stared at the receipt, not quite believing what I saw. An ugly thought occurred—what if Melanie, pretending to be me, had rented the box. What if she'd applied for that credit line? How would she have gotten access to my personal information? Why would she do it?

I knew one thing—I had to see what was in that box. This didn't look good, but I didn't want to draw any conclusions until then.

The phone rang. Faintly, I heard the answering machine's recorded message, a pause, and then tones. Realizing it must be Melanie, checking for messages, I snatched the phone up.

"Hello? Hello?" I said. No response. Only charged silence, then the mechanical clicks and pops of disconnection.

"Damn it," I said. I hung up and tried *69, but it wouldn't go through. So much for that.

The phone was a cordless with caller ID built in. The last caller was *Unknown*. Helpful. I fiddled with the buttons and managed to find out that someone named Bruce Schaeffer called a couple of days ago. The name sounded familiar, and I made a note of it.

I examined the address book again. It had occurred to me that Melanie might be staying with a friend or had told someone else where she was going. I flipped through it quickly. None of the names in it meant anything to me except Donna's.

If I took the address book, was I disturbing a crime scene? I didn't know for sure that this was a crime scene. Finding Melanie might be as easy as making a few phone calls. And if I found her, I'd advise her to go to the police. So I was doing the police a favor by taking it. That's what I told myself. I stowed the book in my purse, along with the envelope.

I locked up behind me when I left and replaced the key under the mat. The early evening sky was a light bluish-gray haze. The humid air felt like warm Jell-O against my skin.

It was after hours at the post office so first thing in the morning, I'd check the box. As I headed home, I remembered who Bruce Schaeffer was—Tom Garvey had moved in with him after Melanie kicked him out. He called a few days ago, after Tom died. Why would he call Melanie? Could they have started a relationship? Maybe after she broke up with Tom. Maybe before. Stranger things have happened.

I pulled over and looked up Schaeffer's address in Melanie's file. He was a few minutes away. It was a long shot, but I could at least ask if he knew where Melanie was.

φ φ φ

Schaeffer lived in what was euphemistically known as "affordable" apartments, literally on the other side of the tracks.

The look-alike buildings were brick boxes—16 units to a box—with shutterless windows as stark as lidless eyes. The lot was full, but I managed to find a space at the far end, near a Dumpster that smelled like something died in it. I parked, walked to his building, and clanked up the metal stairs.

I heard the banging long before I reached the third floor—someone pounding on a door. The chances it was Schaeffer's were only one in sixteen, but sure enough that's where she was. With odds like those, I should have been playing the horses at Laurel Racetrack instead of looking for leads on a missing client.

The woman was taking a break when I got there, leaning against Schaeffer's door, her face twisted into a scowl. She was about my age, short and rail thin, wearing a halter top, cutoffs, and red plastic flip-flops with butterflies on them. Her light brown hair was pulled back, held loosely with one of those hair clips that look like something you'd use to seal a bag of potato chips. She glared at me, as if I were to blame for her problems.

"No one home?" I asked.

"Oh, probably there is," she said, in a dull voice. "Bastard isn't answering." She pounded the door again, several times. I was surprised her fist didn't leave dents. Finally, she swore and flipped the bird at whoever might be inside.

"I wouldn't waste my time," she said, and flounced off before I could think of a reply. After a few moments, I knocked on the door, more softly. Schaeffer might have been there, but not answering. In the mood the woman before me had been in, I wasn't sure I blamed him.

As I waited, the door to the adjoining apartment opened a crack. A red-faced, balding man in boxers and one of those ribbed tank tops reserved for guys over seventy peered at me with impassive, bloodshot eyes.

"Hi," he said. He had a breathy voice. The smell of alcohol and garlic wafted toward me.

"Hello."

"Quite a scene."

"You noticed, huh?"

"Been noticing lots of stuff. This place is turning into Grand Central Station. Dangerous, too. You know, just this week, they found a man shot to death in there."

So Tom died in the apartment. "How awful," I said.

He belched loudly. "You bet it is."

More alcohol and garlic. I tried not to breathe too deeply.

He rambled on about our horrible society, and how no one is safe anymore. I smiled and nodded politely, and was about to excuse myself when he said, "You looking for Bruce? He's probably working out."

"Oh, right," I said. "Now, what was the name of that gym?"

"Kent's Gym. Right down 197."

I snapped my fingers. "Of course. Kent's Gym. Thanks."

Creepy guy. I could feel him staring after me as I walked downstairs.

The Mustang coughed to life with some encouraging gas pedal footwork on my part. I couldn't make a left when I hit the main road, so I went right and maneuvered over quickly to pull a U-turn at the next median break.

Behind me, someone honked his horn, long and loud. I looked back and saw a big, black car with dark windows trying to move to the left lane, holding up traffic in the process. I could picture a blue-haired lady or an old man in a hat hunched behind the wheel. I made the U-turn and noticed the black car did the same.

Out of idle curiosity, I kept my eye on the car. It was a Lincoln, gleaming like it had just been driven from the dealer's. I turned in at the entrance to the parking lot, watching to see if the Lincoln followed. It did.

Could it be following me? Why? Nerves, I thought. The heat must be getting to me.

Kent's Gym was in an old shopping center on Route 197 with a discount grocery and a place that sold ninety-nine-cent greeting cards. I wove through the lot and found a space near the gym. As I was putting the car's roof up, I saw the Lincoln again. It came down the aisle, at a leisurely pace and with a slight bobbing motion, as if it were floating. Maybe it was my imagination, but it seemed to slow a little as it neared me. The big car had a gaudy, chrome hood ornament and chrome trim. Something about the design suggested a rolling, black casket. I shivered and my skin popped goose bumps, despite the evening's warmth.

I also noticed it had New York tags.

The car glided away, never stopping, back to the street, where it merged into traffic and disappeared into the evening haze.

Chapter FOUR

The front of Kent's Gym was a huge plate-glass window with treadmills and cross-trainers lined up so the whole world could admire the sweaty backsides of everyone using them. The ambiance was chilly and loud, overrun with a post-work-hours crowd that was busy flexing and extending its way to better health on various weight machines. ESPN and MTV competed on two TV sets. In the free weights section, a radio played head-banging music, and a man doing bench presses grunted so loudly with each rep, you would have thought he was giving birth.

I had no idea what Schaeffer looked like, so I asked a young girl reading at the front desk whether he was there. "Wow, he's popular tonight," she said. She had short, spiky black hair and marble green eyes, which did a quick sweep around the room. "He was just here, talking to someone. They might have gone back to the exercise room."

"OK if I take a look?"

"Sure," she said, like she was surprised I asked. She pointed me toward a hall off the main gym and delved again into her paperback.

I walked down the short hall, past some closed offices, toward the entrance to the dark exercise room. As I approached, a woman inside the room yelled, "You bastard!"

"Keep it down, would you?" a man hissed in reply.

Casually, I leaned against the wall near the entrance, as if waiting for someone, then stole a quick peek inside. Three people were in there—two women and one man. One of the women glared at the man. The second woman watched them. It was hard to see their faces, since the only light came from a walk-in storage closet across the room. But I recognized Miss Anger Management in the halter top.

"You're lying," she said.

"Why would I lie about such a thing?" he said.

"He can't be dead. You son of a bitch. You're just trying to protect him."

"We're going to get kicked out if you don't shut the hell up."

In the gloom, I made out her expression in profile, a mixture of disbelief and rage. For a moment, she was still. Then she threw herself at the man, wailing and pounding his chest like an infant having a temper tantrum.

The man was tall and well-built. He seemed able to take it, but he was struggling to catch her flailing arms. The other woman kept taking hesitant steps toward them, then back.

The man finally got hold of each of her wrists. She tried to move them and screeched when she couldn't, then hurled a string of expletives at him that could have peeled paint from the walls. I kept expecting someone to come running to see what was going on, but I guess all the noise up front drowned it out.

Eventually, she stopped. She stood there, glaring at the man and sniffling.

He waited a few moments, then let go of her. "Don't ever do that again," he said.

"Men." She hurled the word at him like an accusation. "I hate you. All of you." She marched toward the door. I went back to leaning casually, and she stormed past without even a glance in my direction.

There was a quieter exchange I couldn't make out between the other two. After a few seconds, I went inside.

The man had close-cropped, dark hair, and a beefy triangle of torso, with broad, well-developed shoulders tapering down to a trim tummy and hips. He surveyed me with a puzzled, wary expression.

"Bruce Schaeffer?" I asked.

"Who wants to know?"

"I'm Sam McRae. Melanie Hayes' attorney."

He gave me a cold stare. "Well, that's nice. What the hell do you want?"

I sensed he would have been less polite if I'd been a guy. He had a round, boyish face, but he was no pushover. His arms were corded with muscle. His yellow T-shirt hugged tight, revealing a ripple of perfect abs.

The woman stood off to the side. Her back was to the storage closet, so her face was in shadow, but the light played off her tousled, honey-blonde hair. She had a chunky frame squeezed into a pair of jeans and a skin-tight shirt with a scoop neck that revealed an awning of cleavage.

"I've been having a hard time reaching Melanie," I said. "I wondered if you might know where she is."

"Are you shittin' me?"

"You haven't by any chance seen her? Or spoken to her?" The caller ID had clearly shown his number. I wanted to ask him why, but I didn't want to get into how I knew about the call.

His mouth twisted into a contemptuous grin. "Like I have any reason to talk to that bitch after what she did to Tom."

"She wouldn't have thrown him out if he hadn't hit her," I said.

"Throwing him out did him a favor. I'm talking about how she whacked him."

"Hold on," I said. "You don't know she did that."

"Right." He muttered something that sounded like "fucking lawyers," and then said, "Excuse me," and walked off.

I watched him leave, then turned to the woman. "That went well."

She smiled. "He's a little sensitive about Tom right now." She had a three-pack-a-day voice. "They were friends. And he found the body in his own apartment."

"That is horrible," I said, trying to ingratiate myself a little. "I certainly didn't mean to offend."

"You're just doing your job."

"I couldn't help but notice that little scene with the other woman. What was that all about?"

She shrugged. "Beats me. I just work with Bruce."

"Did you know Tom, Ms. …?"

"Rhonda. Rhonda Jacobi."

As she stepped forward, I got a better look at her face and flinched when I saw the scars. Plastic surgery had smoothed some of the damage, but the right side of her face carried the evidence of burns. Tragic in itself, but even more so when you looked at the other side, which was flawless. I felt awful about my instinctive reaction, but either she hadn't seen it or chose to ignore it.

"I know he was friends with Bruce," she said. "Can't tell you much else."

"So I guess you wouldn't know where Melanie is."

She chuckled. "I don't even know who she is."

"Well, thanks anyway."

"Sure."

I still wanted to know why Bruce called Melanie if he hated her so much. Of course, it could have been a mistake. Maybe he realized he'd dialed the wrong number and hung up.

φ φ φ

I drove past the storefronts on Main Street toward home. I liked living and working on Main Street, because it represented old Laurel, with its little shops in brick buildings—the meat market, the pizza place, the comic book store. Off the main road, the residential sections were mostly old Victorians with front porches and cozy brick ramblers. Throwbacks to the old days, before the malls and the plasterboard housing started sprouting like weeds.

The street was quiet, except outside Mitchie's Restaurant, where the soaring sounds of blues from an electric guitar pierced the night. I drove another block and turned in at the entrance to my garden apartment complex. My luck was good. There was a spot in front of my building.

I didn't see him at first. I was climbing the flight up to my landing, when he poked his head around the end of the balustrade and said, "Hi, Sam."

"Jesus, Ray," I said, putting a hand to my chest. "You took ten years off my life."

"I'm sorry."

"What are you doing here?"

Ray Mardovich got up, brushing off his Dockers. He smiled in a self-mocking way, looking abashed.

"I just wanted to see you," he said.

I shook my head in disbelief. "Did it not occur to you to call?"

"I tried. Where have you been?"

"Here and there. I've had a strange day." For a moment, I toyed with the notion of telling him I was too tired to invite him in, but he'd come more than 20 miles from Mitchellville in central P.G. County to see me.

"It's been a while," I said, stalling.

He reached out and tentatively touched my arm.

I frowned, and he withdrew his hand.

"I know," he said. "It's been difficult."

"So ... Helen's out of town again, and you got bored?"

"I deserve that," he said.

"I won't argue the point." The regret in his hazel eyes looked real. "Would you like a drink?"

"Sure."

We went inside, and I got Ray a beer. I don't usually drink, but I keep it on hand for the occasional guest. That night, I decided to join him.

I had known Ray for years. He was a prosecutor with the state's attorney. I met him while I was with the public defender's office, my first job out of law school. Our affair started six months ago, after a very boring bar association function. He'd been drinking heavily. I had no such excuse. I guess I could blame it on months of abstinence and the lack of a steady male companion for the past few years. Maybe I was looking for what Erica Jong once called the "zipless fuck." Whatever it was, somehow our one-nighter turned into a series of trysts, whenever and however we could manage it.

The last one had been two months ago, and I was starting to wonder if things were winding down between us. Thing was, that whole time, I couldn't bring myself to call or e-mail him. At first, I thought of calling, but as time passed, I thought better of it. I didn't want to be a pain. If it was over, fine. It's not like I expected this thing to last forever. That didn't make it hurt any less though. I also didn't know where it left our friendship, and for some reason, I was afraid to bring that up.

"I didn't see you at the mixer today," I said.

"I had a case and someone else drew the short straw." He grinned.

"To the public sector," I said, raising my bottle in toast. "And not having to market your services. Mind if I turn on the game?"

"Do I ever?"

We watched the Orioles play mediocre ball, sipping beer and exchanging thoughts on how they could improve their chances of getting to the playoffs, short of firing the entire team.

"You came quite a ways to drink beer and watch baseball," I said.

"I didn't come here just for that."

"Oh, I can imagine."

He shot me a glance. "I missed you."

"I've missed you, too." I wanted to say so much more. *I've missed you, but you're married. You've got a family. I can't depend on you to be there for me if I need you.* Instead, I said, "What if I'd brought home a date?"

I saw a brief flash of surprise. Then he laughed. "That could have been awkward."

"Not that there have been all that many," I conceded. Actually, there'd been none.

"I've been thinking about leaving the state's attorney," he said. "Opening my own office."

"Really? You've been there a long time, but I always thought you were happy."

"I don't know. Maybe it's burnout. I think it's time for me to make a move of some sort."

"It's a big decision," I said. "It means you have to go to those mixers you hate on a more regular basis."

"You manage it."

"Yeah, after I take drugs to suppress my gag reflex."

"Maybe I just need to get out of criminal law. Try something else that might lead to an in-house position with a company."

"Regular pay," I said. "Regular hours."

"Some places let you have your own practice, as long as it doesn't conflict with the work you do for them. I could start small, doing stuff for fun on the side."

Like us, I thought. *Fun on the side.* "It's a plan. Maybe a better plan than mine. I guess I just had to get out on my own, win or lose."

"I admire your courage."

We looked at each other for a long time. He reached out and stroked my arm, then drew me toward him and kissed me lightly. When we separated, he looked guilty.

"I really didn't come here just … for this. I really have missed you, but if you want me to go—"

I threw my arms around him and plastered my mouth against his. Our lips were still grinding together as we undressed each other. When our clothes were off, I shoved the coffee table over with one foot for more room. An unread stack of bar association magazines and bulletins spilled onto the floor.

"Get on top," he whispered. We clambered to find a good position on the sofa, while Oscar watched us idly from the other side of the room. The announcer was screaming something about line drives as I put him inside me. Ray's hands touched my breasts and squeezed.

Here we go again, I thought. Were we doomed to repeat this exercise in another two months? Or would it take longer next time? For some reason, it struck me as funny, and I laughed.

"What?" Ray asked.

"Nothing," I said, breathlessly. I hooked my hands around his shoulders and humped with all I had.

Later, as Ray and I held each other, my thoughts turned to Melanie. I wondered how I could possibly help her when I couldn't help myself.

Chapter FIVE

Saturday morning is one of the few times I find driving on
Route 1 bearable. No traffic to speak of, so there's plenty of
room to maneuver around the potholes and bumps and scars in
a road that hasn't been paved in God knows how long.
Normally, Route 1 is like one of those driver's ed movies—cars
making sudden lane changes, darting out randomly from hidden
entrances, left and right. That morning though, I cruised past
the shopping centers of Beltsville, sailed right through the two
sets of lights at Rhode Island Avenue, where traffic usually
snarls, and breezed into College Park without even getting stuck
behind a Metrobus.

I was up early because I'd awakened at four that morning
with Ray on my mind for the first time in almost a month. I'd
thought about him quite a bit during the month after we last saw
each other. When I didn't hear from him, I decided I had a
choice between driving myself crazy and not thinking about
him. I chose the latter.

After an hour of alternately staring at the ceiling and the
inside of my eyelids, I figured it was time to rise and shine, or at
least rise. I showered, fed Oscar, scarfed down a bowl of
Cheerios, and brewed a double-strength cup of dark roast to go.
Then I grabbed the P.O. Box key and headed out.

The post office was on Calvert Road where it dead-ended at the railroad tracks. My route took me past the University of Maryland, my alma mater, a hilly green sweep of campus dotted with colonial brick buildings. Across Route 1 from the campus, the matching brick buildings of fraternities lined a horseshoe-shaped street. Calvert was a residential road that connected with the old U.S. highway in the nerve center of the college town where the bars were. They used to have lines out the door when you could drink beer at eighteen in Maryland. Now, the drinking age was twenty-one. Some of the bars closed, but the rest hung on, continuing to do a solid business with a still young-looking crowd.

I turned onto Calvert, and after countless stop signs, reached the post office. It was a few minutes before ten, so I listened to the car radio, tapping my fingers to the music on the wheel and feeling highly caffeinated blood coursing through my veins. At ten on the dot, they unlocked the front door and I went inside.

At the box, I paused before inserting the key and opening the little door.

Two letters were inside. Again, I hesitated before reaching for them. It's like I expected someone to run up and slap cuffs on me if I did. For checking my own P.O. Box that I didn't know I had, for God's sake.

Neither letter had my name on it. One was a piece of junk for "Boxholder." The other bore the name of Gregory Knudsen.

That guy the FBI man mentioned. What did he have to do with Tom and Melanie?

Maybe Knudsen was the identity thief. Could he have been working with Tom Garvey? Or Melanie? The box was in my legal name, clearly a woman's name, but apparently, other people could have mail delivered to it.

I still didn't have any answers. I was only assuming the P.O. Box was connected with my credit situation, but I couldn't think of any other reason for it.

I looked at the envelope again. Just a regular white business envelope. No return address. A New York City postmark from a couple of weeks ago.

I considered opening it, but that was tampering with someone else's mail, a federal offense. Wonderful. I checked the flap. Someone had done a crummy job of sealing it, only licking the middle. One slip of the thumb and ...

Reluctantly, I put the envelope back in the box. It could be evidence and was not my mail. I probably shouldn't have this box key, I thought.

I didn't really want to talk to the postal clerk—what would I say? The best place to go with this was the cops, but I didn't feel like getting into it with them either. They'd ask a lot of annoying questions, like, "Why didn't you call us when you saw her apartment was tossed?"

I wasn't quite sure. Maybe I was afraid they'd find something incriminating. Maybe it was the fact that I wouldn't have been there to begin with, if it hadn't been for Donna. Anyway, I made a command decision not to call, not sure of the ethical aspects, but based on my gut. So now what?

I decided my best bet was to put the key back where I found it. I didn't want to impede a police investigation, but I had no duty to assist them either. After I returned the key, I could check with Derry, see if they had searched Melanie's place while I had it, and come clean if I had to. He wouldn't like it, but I didn't think it would put me any higher on his shit list than I already was.

φ φ φ

At Melanie's apartment, I let myself in as before. I went to the bedroom and replaced the key and receipt. I was on my way out when I noticed a box on the dining room table.

It was the kind of box you might want to use for moving or storing files—I know, because it actually was full of files. Printed on the side was *Lobkowicz* along with a fancy crest of some sort. If it had been there the day before, I would have noticed.

The folders had names on them and were filed in alphabetical order. I checked one at random. It held correspondence with a bank, something about establishing a credit line.

I slid the folder back into place. I didn't want to go any farther, but I couldn't stop now. I had to check the ones beginning with *M*.

Malone, Martinez, Mazzuli. Then McCabe, McNally. And there it was.

I pulled out the file with my name on it and found the paperwork for my ten-thousand-dollar line of credit. Shit. Less than 24 hours ago, someone had left that box. The someone who'd tried to rip me off.

On my way out, I checked the answering machine. No messages, but Bruce Schaeffer's number was on her caller ID again. He had called at 11:24 p.m., long after I spoke to him. Interesting. Her mailbox hadn't been touched. Her red car was in the same spot.

Anyone could have brought that box in. The key wasn't hard to find. Or maybe the locks were picked.

Why did Bruce phone Melanie again? Was there a connection between his call and the box's appearance? Was it a coincidence?

I wondered how many of the questions Melanie could answer.

φ φ φ

I spent a lot of time that weekend phoning people in Melanie's book. In an attempt at efficiency, I ignored the professional entries—doctors, dentists—and anything identified by an institutional name only. As for the rest, I figured I'd start with *A* and keep going.

Personal phone books have this tendency to collect names the way furniture collects dust and, in my quest, many of those names were about as useless. Some people I called weren't home—I left messages when I could. Some hadn't seen Melanie for years, and some barely knew her to begin with. A couple of people knew her from school, some from the bank. They expressed concern, but couldn't help me. I kept going.

By Monday, I'd slogged through to the *Ms*. I'd developed a short explanatory speech that sounded stale by the third call. I got all sorts of reactions, from skepticism to concern, hostility to apathy. I felt sorry for telemarketers. I was glad to stop and turn my attention back to legal work.

I was wrapping up for the day, when I heard a knock.

"Yes?" I said.

The door opened and a man I didn't recognize stuck his head inside. The disembodied head wore a shock of light brown hair and a genial expression.

"Excuse me, Ms. McRae? I wonder if I could have a moment of your time."

I got up and approached him. "For a consultation?" If he was a potential client, the answer was *yes*. If he was a salesman, my preference was to beat feet home to some take-out Chinese and the ball game.

The door opened all the way, revealing a sturdy frame—not fat, not skinny, maybe a slight beer belly—clothed in a pair of chinos, a Madras shirt, and moccasins. He stuck out a squarish hand.

"My name is John Drake. I'm a friend of Melanie Hayes' parents. Were you busy? I could come back."

"No, that's OK." Feeling curious, I invited him in.

Drake relaxed into a guest chair, crossing a leg over one knee. He looked a bit like an overgrown version of a kid in a Rockwell painting, complete with cheek of tan and unruly cowlick.

"Melanie's mother called a few days ago. Her folks are concerned, because they've been told she's missing. Since I live in the area, they asked me to try to contact her."

"Oh?" The wariness that rose in me was almost palpable. "How do you know her parents?"

"I've known Melanie since she was a kid."

"That's interesting." He looked like he was close to Melanie's age. "So they looked you up? Or have you kept in touch with them since they moved to New Mexico?"

Drake smiled broadly. His teeth were as even and white as Chiclets. "Arizona," he corrected me. "They live in Arizona."

"Oh, yeah. Right."

Drake's smile faded, but his green eyes continued to look amused. "I'm doing her folks a favor."

"Sure. But I don't know how I can help you."

"I understand from someone at the bank that you're her attorney."

That could only be Donna.

"Correct," I said. "You'll understand if I'm a little protective when it comes to a client."

"Certainly. Really, I have no dark motives." He spread his hands, as if he were opening himself like a book. "I'm just trying to help."

"Unfortunately, I have no idea where she is."

"Ah." He looked terribly disappointed. "I was hoping you might have heard from her."

"I haven't."

"She didn't give you a possible alternate address or phone number to contact her at?"

I shook my head.

"Not to impose, but could you possibly recheck your file?" Something seemed to catch in his throat, and he began to cough.

"No need," I said. "I've been trying to find Melanie myself. Believe me, if I had a lead in my file, I would know about it."

Drake coughed harder. "Excuse me," he said. "Got a ... bit of a tickle. Have any water?"

I inclined my head. "There's a water cooler down the hall. Help yourself."

He got up and left, hacking loudly. Maybe he really did have a tickle. Or maybe it was an old trick. It was a short hallway, but it still gave a person time to get something from your desk or off your Rolodex. I had two people pull that on me, using different ruses—a reporter who was looking for a name and phone number, and a prospective client who lifted my wallet. Fool me twice, shame on me all over. Maybe I was being paranoid. Still, something wasn't right with this guy, although I wondered what he could be looking for that he'd be able to find in that little bit of time.

I decided to meet him at the door on his way back.

"I'm afraid I'm going to have to cut this short," I said. "I have plans."

"That's quite all right. I appreciate your time." I don't think he believed me any more than I did him.

"Perhaps if you gave me a phone number," I said. "If I hear anything, I could call you."

His expression was neutral, but the eyes still seemed amused. "Good idea." He felt his shirt pocket. "I'm afraid I don't have anything to write with."

I got a pad and pen from my desk and he wrote a number down. After he left, I waited at the window until I saw him heading down the front walk. Then I got on the phone to Donna.

"John Drake?" she said. "Never heard of him."

"This guy says he's known Melanie since they were kids."

"That's news to me."

"And you never told him that I was Melanie's attorney?"

"I've never even met him. Oh, Sam." She paused. "You don't suppose that could be … that couldn't be the one the police were talking about, could it? The dangerous man?"

"I don't know." I didn't think so, but my pulse had quickened. Could that really be Stavos?

"He didn't seem dangerous," I said, "but that doesn't mean a thing, does it?"

"Sam, did you have a chance to run by Melanie's?"

I paused. "Oh, yeah. She wasn't home." I decided to leave it at that.

"I'm so worried."

So was I. If this was the man Jergins was talking about, he'd managed to find out I was Melanie's attorney. And if he was that dangerous, would he be satisfied asking a few questions? I didn't think so. I just wondered what his next move would be.

Chapter SIX

Detective Derry stopped by the office the next day. Jergins was with him, looking sullen and officious.

"Things aren't looking good for your client," Derry said.

"Now what?"

"Garvey's body was found in his apartment. A witness says Ms. Hayes was there that weekend, the weekend he was shot."

That creepy neighbor of Schaeffer's, I thought. "So?"

"Didn't she have a protective order against this guy? Why would she want to see him?"

It was a fair question. "I don't know, but it doesn't prove she killed him."

Derry took a deep breath. "I didn't say it proved anything."

"Maybe it was someone who looked like Melanie."

"Anything's possible. The witness identified her from a photo we found in her apartment."

"You searched her place?"

He nodded. "Yesterday."

He didn't mention the box or the state of the apartment, and I wasn't going to bring it up.

"Was there any reason for that, other than a witness' statement?"

"Fingerprints," Derry said. "We found her prints at the scene."

"How do you know they're hers?" I had to ask.

"The bank where she works routinely takes its employees prints."

I was at a loss to understand or explain it, but I didn't owe anyone any explanations. "What do you want from me?"

"I just wanted to let you know we're getting a warrant for Ms. Hayes' arrest," Derry said.

I nodded. What could I say? I'd have done the same thing in their place.

"So if you have any knowledge of Ms. Hayes' whereabouts, now would be the right time to tell us," Jergins barked.

I could understand if the FBI didn't offer courses in diplomacy, but I was starting to wonder if it should. Even Derry didn't look happy about Jergins' outburst.

"If I had any knowledge of Ms. Hayes' whereabouts," I said, keeping my voice deliberately calm. "I would have told you by now."

Jergins squinted and scowled at me.

"We thought it would be a good idea to check with you," Derry said, sounding almost conciliatory. "Just in case."

"I understand. What about the murder weapon? Were her fingerprints on that?"

"We'll discuss that at the appropriate time, Ms. McRae," Jergins said, interrupting.

Derry's eyes slid Jergins' way. His cheeks reddened, and I didn't think it was from embarrassment.

"Really?" I said. "And when did you start working for the homicide unit?"

"There's an appropriate time and place for everything." Jergins' face was tight, making his big ears stand out even more. "We'll discuss the murder weapon at that time and place."

"Now, I wonder when that would be. Maybe at the sentencing hearing?"

Derry turned away. I didn't know, but I could have sworn he stifled a smile.

"With all due respect, Ms. McRae," Jergins said. "We don't know that Ms. Hayes will hire you to represent her."

"Why not?"

"You represented her on a domestic violence matter. That doesn't mean she'll want you for this."

I looked at Derry. He was staring at something on my desk. I realized it was Melanie's address book, still sitting beside the phone.

"As far as I'm concerned," I said, addressing my comments to both men, trying to bring Derry back into the conversation, "she's still my client."

"Mr. Garvey's dead," Jergins said. "The case is moot, and you know it."

"Sure, the court case is moot, but I don't consider the *entire* matter closed," I said. "After all, your interest in her was sparked by that case. I haven't closed the file. So it's still an open case, from my standpoint, and she's still my client." Not bad, I thought. Pretty smooth, even.

Derry kept looking at the book. The plain, dark cover had nothing to connect it with Melanie, but I couldn't remember if her name was on the inside.

Jergins sneered. "Very convenient. Keeps that attorney-client privilege intact."

"You know the privilege doesn't let me help clients commit crimes."

"I know that. Maybe we should get a warrant and make sure you know that, too."

I gaped at him.

Derry coughed. "Can I talk to you a minute?" he said to Jergins. "Excuse us."

They left the office. A few minutes later, Derry returned, alone. "He's going to wait in the car."

"Is this supposed to be some weird variation on 'good cop, bad cop'? What the hell's his problem anyway?"

Derry shrugged. "Lacks a few social skills. Guess he has a thing about defense lawyers."

"You think?"

"He also thinks you know something you're not telling us."

"But you know better, right?"

"I think you're telling us everything you know," he said. "I certainly hope so."

"I am." He seemed to have lost interest in the address book. Guilt gnawed at me, but the book didn't have any answers, at least not yet.

"The man he mentioned, Christof Stavos," he said. "He is dangerous."

"I know. It's been bothering me. You really think he might hurt Melanie?"

"It's possible. Or maybe you."

"Why would he have any interest in me?"

"I don't know. Maybe for the same reason that Jergins thinks you're holding something back."

"Christof Stavos has a thing about defense attorneys, too?"

Derry toyed with his shirt cuff. "Were you talking to someone at Bruce Schaeffer's apartment?"

That blabbermouthed neighbor must have told them about me. I never gave my name, but Derry may have recognized the description.

"Yeah, I went there. I was hoping Schaeffer would know something about Melanie. Didn't pan out." I paused, then laughed uncomfortably. "There is something else. It's kind of silly."

"Go ahead."

I told him about the black Lincoln and the visit from John Drake the day before. Derry's brow furrowed, the lines growing deeper as I spoke.

"You didn't get the tag on the car, did you?" he asked.

I shook my head. "I'm sorry. I didn't even think of it."

"That's OK."

"Another thing—I think that guy Drake gave me a fake name. I checked him out in some of the Internet directories and got nothing."

"I think you're right." Derry paused and arched an eyebrow. "And I think, whoever he is, he has a sense of humor."

"How's that?"

Derry smiled. "You're probably a little too young to remember the show *Secret Agent Man*. John Drake was the name of the main character."

"And they say television isn't educational."

Derry stole a glance at me. The look suggested we were just two human beings talking. No ghosts haunting us anymore. However, the moment passed.

With the usual formality, Derry shook my hand. "If you hear anything, please let us know. Please keep what we said in mind."

"Sure."

After he left, I wondered what I'd gotten into. I should have given Derry the address book.

I think I would have, except that Melanie was still my client. I wasn't going to run out on a client, not without getting her side first. Something about the setup didn't seem right. Killing Garvey, then leaving a box of incriminating files in her own apartment made zero sense to me.

As for Stavos, I didn't know much about the Mob, but I was under the impression they didn't kill people without a reason. When it came to this case, I felt like I was too clueless for them to bother with me.

Since I had no meetings or court dates, I dug back into Melanie's phone book with renewed vigor. A person didn't just disappear. They left traces somewhere. If she was with a friend, I should be able to find that friend. If she was at a motel, she'd eventually run out of money and have to turn to someone she knew. Donna would have been a logical person, but whether it was shame or pride, something was keeping Melanie from seeking her out.

I stuck with it and managed to make it all the way through *S*. A lot of the calls were long-distance. Either Melanie had traveled a lot or her friends did. She seemed to know people all over the U.S. and even someone in Canada. I figured I'd rest up before I tackled the multitude of *T*s—Thompson, Tillman, Toohey …

I did some other work and a few administrative chores then left the office around five thirty.

At home, I fed Oscar, then took an evening ride on my old Schwinn. I'd been trying to exercise more regularly, do at least five miles every couple of days. Lately, I'd slacked off a bit, because of the heat and humidity. After the workout, I lugged the bike upstairs, sweaty and panting. Maybe a bit more diligence was in order.

The food situation was reaching a critical point, but I managed to throw together a tuna salad with dill pickle slices for dinner, which I ate while watching the news. The O's weren't playing. TV sucked. I thumbed through some magazines, then went onto the balcony. The sun had set, and the air was as moist and heavy as a wet blanket. Like a locker room, only filled with the pungent smell of cut grass and impending rain. Now and then, I heard the low rumble of distant thunder and saw lightning flicker in the dark sky.

I wished Ray were with me. I knew that wasn't possible. When those months had gone by and he hadn't called, at first missing him was like a chronic ache in my belly. I forced myself to forget. Then he showed up at my door. Now the ache was back. And again, he couldn't be here.

I liked living alone, doubted if I could abide sharing my space with anyone, but sometimes I wondered. If I dropped dead tomorrow, who would care? Maybe a few people, but …

Still things could be worse. What if I were Melanie? Apart from my problems, maybe that was one reason I was so interested in finding her. She was all alone like me—probably scared shitless and in over her head.

Was that where I was with Ray? Over my head? I felt a wave of self-pity wash over me.

"Damn it," I said. "Snap the fuck out of this."

It was time for drastic measures. I marched straight to the fridge and went for the chocolate chip cookie dough ice cream. Unfortunately, the carton contained about two spoonfuls, tops.

"Shit." I sighed. I didn't really want to go out, but unless I provisioned up, my next dinner was going to be a shriveled hot dog that I probably should have thrown out months ago or another Lean Cuisine. Plus, I needed that ice cream, for medicinal purposes.

I grabbed my purse and headed out. As I walked, I realized a car was pulling up beside me. It had a garish hood ornament. The Lincoln's back doors were already open and two men were coming at me when I turned to run. I didn't get far. They each took an arm and dragged me toward the car, one clapping a hand over my mouth before I could utter a peep.

My head felt light, and my stomach had that hard knot you get before you throw up. My pulse raced. I squirmed, but they had my arms locked in place. I kicked as hard as I could, connecting with one guy's knee. He yelped in pain and his grip on my arm loosened enough for me to wrench free and scratch the other one's face. As he cried out, his hand dropped from my mouth, although he continued to hold my other arm tight.

"Help!" I hollered at the top of my lungs. I tried to pull away from him. "Help!"

More noise, talking, footsteps behind me. Somebody grabbed my shoulders. Before I could yell again, I got a punch in the gut. I couldn't breathe, talk, or move.

"Bitch," a man said, as they dragged me into the car.

Someone blindfolded me, and we took off.

Chapter SEVEN

By the time I recovered my wind, they'd gagged me and tied my hands behind my back. The rope was tight, making my wrists hurt. Having my arms stretched back was awkward, forcing me to use muscles I'd not used in ages. The car's air conditioning was on full blast. I was freezing and sweating like a pig. On the whole, it was not an ideal arrangement.

They took me somewhere. I can't tell you where. I can't even tell you how long it took. A blindfold takes away all sense of place and time. Being terrified doesn't make things much better.

When we finally got to wherever the hell we went, they guided me out of the car with hands gripping both my arms. We marched a few yards, then stopped. I heard the jingle of keys. No one spoke.

A door opened and we went inside. The floor was hard and the only sound was the faint echo of our footsteps. We walked until we reached another door. More walking, then up a short flight of steps. Despite my fear, I was amazed at how well my other senses worked, taking up the slack caused by the blindfold. First, a hard floor, then a carpet, now bare floor again. The place felt warm and stuffy, but maybe I was just nervous. The guys holding my arms were firm, but not rough. Not gentle either, but they had no reason to be rough—yet.

They maneuvered me around until I felt something against the back of my knees. One of the men grunted something like "siddown" in my ear. I complied with gratitude. My legs shook. Sweat dripped from my armpits and my stomach was jumpy. I desperately hoped I wouldn't vomit—especially with the gag on.

They bound my legs and took off the blindfold and gag. I was on a stage, facing a dark theater, squinting into two blinding white spotlights. When my eyes adjusted, I could see empty seats. What had I expected, a full house?

"Ms. McRae." A disembodied male voice, electrically amplified, boomed from the dark.

I blinked and waited for more.

"Ms. McRae," the voice repeated in an implacable and monotonous tone. "It's good to meet you."

I didn't trust myself to say anything, so I nodded.

"I'm sorry about the inconvenience. It's important you know we're serious."

No shit, I thought. I licked my lips, but my mouth had gone so dry it was a wasted gesture.

"You do realize that?"

I worked my mouth again and managed to say, "Yes." It sounded like I'd swallowed ground glass.

"Good. Let's get down to business then," the robotic voice droned on. "It would be good to do this quickly and painlessly, don't you agree?"

He could have been talking about killing me, for all I knew. I said, "Yes."

"Where is Melanie Hayes, Ms. McRae?"

"I don't know."

"What was that?"

"I don't know." In my peripheral vision, I sensed a presence. A big, heavy, muscle-bound presence.

"Is that your final answer?"

Had I been kidnapped by Regis Philbin? "I just don't—"

Suddenly, I was facing left, my cheek stinging, but I hadn't turned my head—someone had turned it for me. The slap had come fast and from out of nowhere.

"Where is she?"

I tried to catch my breath. "I ... don't know."

Another slap, harder this time. The lights were making my eyes hurt. My head throbbed.

"Where is Melanie Hayes?"

Again, I told him I didn't know. I got a punch in the ribs. Then another.

"Where is she?"

I shook my head. It hurt to breathe now. Another hard slap followed by a punch in the gut. I gasped for air.

"Stop that," the voice commanded. "Give her time."

The muscle man stepped back. I got my time. Then the voice said, "What's your business with Bruce Schaeffer?"

How the hell had Schaeffer gotten into this? "Wanted to ask him some questions."

"About what? What sort of questions?"

"Thought maybe he might know where Melanie is."

Pause. "I'm not sure I believe you."

Hands pulled me from the chair and threw me to the floor. My head hit with a bang. A kick landed in the kidney region of my lower back. I howled as an electric current of pain shot through me.

"What did you talk about, Ms. McRae? Be specific, please. I want details." The voice boomed relentlessly.

"I asked him if he knew where she was," I gasped. "That's all."

"Why would he know?"

"It was a hunch." I said it fast, trying to get it out before the next blow landed. "I'm trying to find her. The police are looking for her. That's all."

I braced myself, waiting for something worse to happen.

The voice was silent. Finally, the man said, "Did Melanie Hayes leave anything with you?"

"No."

"Nothing? Are you sure?"

"No. She didn't give me anything."

"You lying bitch. Talk." This from the muscle man, who kicked me again and again. He slammed me onto my back and with one arm pinned my shoulders down and sat astride my thighs, smashing my bound hands into the hard floor. He stared at me with eyes as devoid of warmth as a shark's. A deep scar ran down his left cheek.

I heard a metallic snick and a switchblade moved into view above my face.

"Tell us, you filthy, lying cunt. Tell us or I'll cut your fuckin' eyes out." The knife hovered over my left eye, then moved in closer.

I whimpered.

"Stop that, you idiot." the voice ordered. "Get off her right now."

I lay there, ready to piss my pants, thinking about spending the rest of my life mutilated or blind. I didn't dare move or breathe. I wanted to pass out.

"I said get off her," the voice commanded.

The muscle man finally withdrew the knife and got up. He seemed reluctant.

I gasped for breath. My body shook uncontrollably.

"If you're lying, Ms. McRae—"

"I'm not," I said in a strangled voice. "I swear."

A long pause. The muscle man continued to stand over me, a dark silhouette against the spotlights. The only sound was his heavy breathing.

"All right. I think you're telling the truth. If I find out you're lying … things won't go so easy next time."

With those words, I knew I was going to live. The blindfold and gag went back on. They untied my feet, helped me up, and half-walked, half-carried me to the car. My head ached where it had hit the floor. The ride home was silent and took forever.

They stopped in front of my building, helped me out, untied my hands and left before I could get the blindfold off. Again, I didn't get the tag number.

I was right about one thing—the Mob didn't kill unless it had to. What I hadn't anticipated was they might beat the crap out of me.

It must have rained while I was gone, although it hadn't cooled things down any. The parking lot was damp, glowing with the reflections of lights on the apartment buildings. Steam rose from the asphalt, creating an outdoor sauna.

For one panicky moment, I thought I'd lost my purse, until I realized it hung from my shoulder. Dazed, I hobbled to my building, but couldn't bring myself to climb the stairs. I sat down to rest. Next thing I knew, I lay on the steps, my head on my arm and my eyes closed. My body felt like one huge bruise. Every breath I took was agony. It even hurt to think.

I heard a door open and close somewhere. I considered moving. Why bother? Footsteps. If they could walk, they could walk around me.

"What the hell?"

A familiar nasal voice. I opened my eyes. I knew this guy. Mid-sixties, hair a glossy, dyed brown, brown eyes and a disgusted expression. My downstairs neighbor, Russell Burke.

"Hi." I tried to push myself upright with little success.

Russell came around and helped me sit up. "What the hell's wrong with you? Are you drunk?"

I shook my head. "No. Drunk would not be it."

"What the hell are you doing lying here on the stairs?"

"Resting." I felt nauseated again. The effort of talking was making me sick. I was thirsty, too. I needed to get to bed.

He scowled. "I hope that crazy fool who left here with his tires squealing wasn't your date. Hey." His look changed to one of concern. "My God, you look pale."

"I feel kind of pale. Ha ... oh, ow." I clutched my rib cage. "Bad move. Worst date of my life. Uh-oh." Things spun, but I caught hold of a step with one hand to steady myself. My tongue felt like a piece of dried leather.

"Sam? Sam?" Russell's voice sounded tinny and far away.

"No problem," I mumbled. "Just get me a gallon of water and a bed, and I'll be fine. Okeydokey?" I grabbed the handrail and, ignoring the pain, pulled myself up. Then I passed out.

Chapter EIGHT

I was in the bottom of a well, looking up. It was night. I could see the stars. I was cold. I was wet. It was a long way to the top. Voices. The sound of voices echoed down the well. They made my head throb.

I tried to yell, but nothing came out.

Someone's beeper went off. Voices and a beeper. They were driving me crazy.

At the top of the well, a woman's face appeared. She smiled at me.

"Melanie?" I called out. "Melanie?"

A spotlight blinded me. Not again. Please, don't hit me again. Please …

"Melanie," I mumbled.

"Shhh. Lie still." Words spoken in a low and reassuring tone. Someone touched my wrist, someone with cool hands. I opened my eyes. I wasn't in a well. I was on my back, a nurse standing beside me. She was taking my pulse. I lifted my head a bit. Curtains hung around me. Where they parted, I could see people in white coats and hospital scrubs. Machines beeped. I put my head back down.

"Hello," I said, the word stumbling off my tongue.

"Hello," she said. She looked me over in a way that was both appraising and concerned. She seemed to exist in a zone of calm, which she shared with me.

"Will I live?" My voice sounded bizarre and unnatural. It seemed to be out of sync with the movements of my mouth. My own voice dubbed into the movie of my life.

She smiled. "I think you have a few more years left in you." Her voice had a Midwestern twang making me think of apple pie.

"Yay. I'm gonna live." My voice came out in a singsong. Far away, someone laughed. Suddenly, I felt very tired. I drifted off into a dreamless sleep.

I woke up again in a hospital room, my mouth so dry, I could have sworn there was dust in it. When I tried to sit up, my head and abdomen protested. It was light out, but it must have been early evening. The TV was turned on low to *Access Hollywood*. Russell slept in a chair.

"Russell?" I croaked. His head snapped up, and he opened his eyes, blinking. He appeared to be as disoriented as I was.

"Oh, thank heavens," he said. He rubbed his face, as if to wipe the fatigue off.

"How long have you been here?"

"Since the ambulance brought you."

I felt swelling in my belly and probed it. Tender. "Where am I?"

"Laurel Hospital."

"You look awful."

He did an exaggerated double take. "You should talk, missy."

I chuckled, then cringed. God, my throat was parched.

"You're kind, Russell. Go home. You shouldn't do this to yourself."

"Who else is there?" he snapped.

He glared at me, in that disapproving way of his, then his look softened. He never stayed mad for long. "I thought it was important for someone to be here when you woke up," he said.

"You're a real friend, you know that?" I whispered.

He stood and walked over to me. "We all need friends." He stroked my hair, looking at me with a mixture of concern, gratitude, and relief.

For a moment, I feared I'd burst into tears.

A nurse came in to take my vitals. She had water. I wanted to chug it all, but she made me sip it. Then a doctor joined us. He said intestinal bleeding caused my abdominal swelling. A bruised kidney was the worst of it. I had a mild concussion and a serious knot on my head. In short, I was extremely lucky.

I felt good, all things considered, until he said they'd probably keep me for at least a week.

"But I've got a business to run," I said. "I can't lie around here for a week. My clients depend on me."

"You're not going to be able to take care of them until you can take care of yourself," the doctor said.

I was so exhausted, I didn't want to think, let alone argue with the guy.

Russell stayed after the medical staff left. "Let me get together with that woman in your office. If there's anything we need to reschedule, we'll handle it."

"OK," I said, forcing myself to remember what I had on my plate for the next few days. No court dates, but there were a few meetings. "Sheila has a spare key to the office. Now, she doesn't work for me, Russell, so don't expect too much from her. My calendar's on the desk. And Jamila's number is in my Rolodex. Maybe she can lend a hand." I lay back on the pillow, my head spinning.

"You've got to relax," Russell directed. "Even after you get out of the hospital, you'll need time to recover."

"Jesus." I always wondered what I'd do if this happened. Self-employed people should always have a back-up plan, someone to turn to if they're incapacitated. I felt as helpless and small as a bug on its back, trying to get upright. I was lucky I had friends I could depend on.

The first few days were tough. Once I got off the painkillers, I started to feel better, but it was still an effort to get around.

Russell brought books and magazines. Jamila stopped by and offered to fill in for me on any cases that needed immediate help. While she took care of the legal minutiae, Russell cleared my calendar of meetings and other stuff for the next few weeks and looked after Oscar. It was both gratifying and nerve-racking. I've never felt such a lack of control.

As the week crawled by, I improved slowly. I took extended walks around the floor as soon as I could, partly out of boredom and partly to show everyone how great I was doing. They wiped me out at first, but I got stronger each time. Near the end of my stay, I won't say I was ready to run a marathon, but I was definitely moving better. I was also anxious to return to the outside world, despite being told by the police when they interviewed me that I should lie low for the immediate future.

When the doctor told me I could go, I almost jumped for joy.

"But you'll have to take it easy," he warned. "Don't push yourself, or you'll end up back here."

"Sure. I understand." Nod and smile, I thought. And get the hell out of here.

Russell picked me up. My calendar was clear for the next two weeks. I expressed my eternal gratitude. When we got to my apartment, I remembered that I needed to buy food. That's what started this whole mess, going out for groceries.

When I mentioned it to Russell, he said, "Stay here. I'll do your shopping."

"Russell, I can do this—"

"Shut the hell up and make a list."

Who was I to argue? After he left, I lay on the couch and watched TV. Same as I could have done at the hospital, but somehow, it made a great deal of difference that I was home.

φ φ φ

The next day, I went to the office. I'd been out a mere week, but it seemed a lot longer. Besides, I couldn't depend on the kindness of friends forever. I needed to check in.

Sheila stopped what she was doing when she saw me. "You're supposed to be resting," she snapped. "What are you doing here?"

"It's just for a little while."

I couldn't believe the fuss Sheila made over me. Even Milt Kressler, my landlord, roused himself from his desk long enough to ask how I was. I assured them I was fine and slipped upstairs to my office as quickly as I could. I would have to remember to come during off-hours next time. Placating them was more exhausting than work.

It felt good to be in my office. Familiar and ordinary. I walked in, switched on my computer, and started through the stacks of mail. Sheila or Jamila had already checked for important-looking stuff and set it aside. I had only a few voice mail messages, and more than a hundred e-mails, mostly junk. There was nothing from Ray.

Stop being such a hardheaded idiot. Pick up the phone and call him, I thought. I got through to his secretary, who said Ray would be gone for the next few days.

"You have a case coming up with him, Sam?" she asked.

"It's not urgent." I kept my voice more matter-of-fact than I felt.

"He took leave on short notice and we scrambled to cover his cases, so I wanted to make sure we hadn't missed yours or something. His wife had to go to San Francisco on business, and he decided to go along at the last minute. Must be nice, huh?"

"Yeah. Must be nice."

I hung up and sat there a while. I had no right to feel angry, sad, or disappointed. I had no rights at all. Finally, I gathered some files and went home.

I spent most of the day doing research, writing letters, and making phone calls. I couldn't just lie around the apartment. When you come down to it, very few things are more therapeutic for me than work.

The next morning, I slept late and made pancakes for breakfast. I was still sore, so I did some light stretching. Don't know if it really helped, but it was nice to know I could do it. I read the paper while sipping my coffee, then did some work, still in my PJs. That only lasted about ten minutes. I changed into shorts and a T-shirt, feeling better for doing so. I can't work in pajamas.

Around ten thirty, I checked my office voice mail. Someone named Jenna Pulaski had left a message earlier that morning. She was one of the people I'd called about Melanie.

I dialed the number she left and got through to her desk at work.

"Oh, hi," she said. "Look, um, something's come up."

"What is it? Have you heard from Melanie?"

"Yes," she said. "She called last night."

I'd begun to think I was about as likely to find Melanie as I was to find the Holy Grail, so she had my full attention. "Where is she?"

"She wouldn't say exactly, but she sounded strange. I told her you called."

"And?"

"And nothing, really. All she could talk about was coming to Chicago."

"What?"

"She said she was in a real bind." Jenna sounded distraught. "She made me promise not to tell anyone. I kept asking her what it was about, but she wouldn't say."

I swore under my breath. "When's she supposed to get there?"

"She's leaving this morning by bus. She may have already left."

"Damn."

"I should have called you last night, but she asked me not to tell anyone she was coming. She was ... very emphatic about that." Jenna paused. "Melanie and I go way back. I'd do anything to help her, but I need to know what's going on."

It was my turn to hesitate. "I don't really want to get into the details. You did the right thing calling me."

"Is she in trouble?"

"Yes. I'm afraid it involves the police."

"The police? Oh, my God."

"Did she say what time she was leaving?"

Jenna sighed. "Not the exact time. I know she's taking Greyhound."

"OK. I really appreciate your calling. I don't mean to cut you off, but I should probably check on whether her bus has left."

"Sure. Wow, I had no idea how serious this was. I can't believe Melanie committed a crime."

"Right now, we don't know that she has," I said. "But going to Chicago is not her best move."

After I hung up, I got onto the Internet. Within minutes, I discovered Greyhound had only two buses going to Chicago from Maryland that morning—one from Silver Spring, the other from Annapolis. Both had already left.

Was Melanie running from the law? From the Mob? Chicago wasn't going to be nearly far enough, in either case. From Chicago, it would be easy to get to Canada. Maybe the plan was to connect with her Canadian friend. But the law had extradition, and the Mob wasn't going to stop at the border if they wanted her.

Why hadn't she called me when Jenna told her I was looking for her? The cynical side of my brain kicked in. What if she planned the entire thing? She could have planned to kill Garvey. She could be using stolen money to bankroll her escape.

But that box of files. Why the hell would she kill Garvey, then leave the files in her apartment? Maybe someone was trying to give her away? Or maybe someone was setting her up?

So far, I had plenty of questions. If I were going to get answers, I'd have to find Melanie.

Chapter NINE

According to the schedules, the buses took circuitous routes through the western Maryland hills, hitting burgs like Frederick and Hagerstown before leaving the state. Around lunchtime, both buses would arrive in Breezewood, Pennsylvania. If I left now and stepped on it, I could beat them there.

I'd been to Breezewood, the "Town of Motels." Nobody lives there. Its sole reason for being is to cater to interstate travelers, with every roadside restaurant, gas station, and budget motel you can imagine, their stilted signs creating a loud and competitive skyline. There was a cafeteria where the buses stopped.

I figured I could manage the four-hour, round-trip drive, despite my aches and pains. I printed out the bus schedules and the map, grabbed my purse, and headed out.

The Mustang had been sitting for more than a week, so it took a couple of tries to start it. On the way to I-95, it ran so rough, I had to brake with one foot and give it gas with the other at stoplights to keep it going. Once I reached the interstate, it was smooth sailing.

I kept checking my rearview mirror for the black Lincoln, but I never saw it. I hoped that meant that it wasn't there.

As the sun got higher, it got hotter. I could see the outlines of puffy clouds and the barest hint of blue sky behind the haze. I kept the convertible top down for the breeze, donning an Orioles cap and sunscreen for protection. By the time I reached Breezewood, I felt windblown and decided to raise the roof for the trip back.

Breezewood was exactly the way I remembered it—ugly and snarled with traffic from the interstate, which literally runs through the town. This makes I-70 the only interstate with a traffic light, as far as I know.

It wasn't hard to find the cafeteria, high on a hill overlooking the jumble and hubbub of commerce below. Several buses had parked diagonally, face in, along the side of the building. Melanie's bus wasn't scheduled to arrive for almost twenty minutes.

Inside, a clattering mass of lunchtime customers filled the industrial-sized dining room. I did a quick tour through the cafeteria and the gift shop. A few women were traveling alone, but none that resembled Melanie. I didn't see her in the bathroom either.

I bought a sandwich and a cup of coffee and took a seat. Another bus must have arrived because a throng of gawky teens came in. Within minutes, they'd formed a queue around the room, while a couple of adults moved back and forth along the line with a supervisory air.

Bus depots get a bad rap, but I thought the cafeteria had an interesting mix of people—different ages, different walks of life. Bus travel is a great equalizer. No first class or coach. No special compartments. Everyone treated the same. A guy with a briefcase here, a family of four there. A couple of elderly women. And two Pennsylvania state troopers.

Bus stops are favorite places for cops to do random drug searches. Breezewood had something of a reputation for that. Maybe these guys had just stopped for coffee. It was also possible the cops in Maryland had asked them to keep a look out for Melanie. It didn't seem likely that Pennsylvania would send officers to Breezewood just for that purpose, but they might be keeping a routine eye out for her.

Thinking it might be best to snag Melanie in the parking lot, I finished eating and wove my way among the tables to the door. Outside, I stood in the shade of a large awning that ran the length of the building to escape the searing heat. According to my watch, the next bus was due in about ten minutes.

After a while, a bus going to Detroit pulled up and wheezed to a stop. The doors opened. Behind the tinted windows, I could make out the passengers rising, getting ready to file off. As I waited, a second bus eased in, two spaces away from the first. This one was en route to Memphis.

Melanie was going to Chicago with a transfer in Cleveland. Either of the buses could have been going through Cleveland, and my schedules didn't tell where they went after that. I kept my eye on both sets of passengers as they disembarked.

Then a third bus appeared, parking several spaces down. Its destination was Des Moines. For all I knew, it was going through Cleveland, too.

"Shit," I said. The passengers spilled out of the first two buses, descending en masse on the cafeteria. I scanned the crowd for a dark-haired, thirtyish woman. I wondered if she might have disguised herself.

The flow of passengers from the third bus joined the others. I tried to keep my eye on everyone, but it was hard. Still no sign of Melanie.

When the last person got off, I walked into the cafeteria. The crowd was thick now. People walked every which way, many joining the long line for food. I looked for the cops. They were at a table eating lunch. Circling the room, I checked the line and the tables. Maybe Melanie had changed her plans. Or maybe she was still on the bus.

I checked the rest room again, then went outside. I checked the Detroit bus first. Then the one to Memphis. Finally, the one to Des Moines.

An elderly man sat up front and a woman nursing an infant was a few rows behind him. I almost missed Melanie. She was way in the back, slouched in her seat, her hair tucked under a baseball cap, wearing sunglasses and gazing out the window. As I walked up the aisle, she turned toward me and did a double take.

"What are you doing here?" she asked, taking off her sunglasses. Her face was pale, and she looked like she hadn't slept in days.

"You have to come back with me."

"Wait a minute. How did you know I was here?"

"I'll tell you later. Right now, we need to get out of here."

"No."

"Yes."

"You don't understand," she protested.

"No, you don't understand." I slid onto the seat beside her and said in a low voice so the others wouldn't hear, "You're in danger. The Mob is after you."

"I know, but who told *you*?"

So she knew about the Mob. "That can wait. We have another problem. The state police are here. They might be looking for you."

"Me? Why?"

She seemed genuinely confused. "I don't know how else to tell you this, so I'll just tell you. The police have a warrant for your arrest in Maryland."

"What?"

"They think you may have murdered Tom Garvey."

Her face went white. "Tom? Tom is … dead? Oh …"

For a moment, I thought she might pass out. "I'm sorry. You didn't know?"

She shook her head.

"You're going to need an attorney," I said. "We can talk about that later. Right now, you have to come back to Maryland. Running away will only make things worse."

Melanie nodded, staring in front of her. "OK," she whispered.

"Let's find the driver, so we can get your luggage."

"It's up there … on the luggage rack," she said. "The black bag."

I looked and found a medium-sized black bag. She had packed it solid and it took a bit of effort to get it down. She continued to stare straight ahead.

"Let's go," I said, tapping her on the shoulder.

"Oh." She grimaced and blurted out, "Oh, God, I don't believe this is happening to me."

The two others in the bus looked at us in alarm. I ignored them and sat next to Melanie. If this was an act, she deserved an Oscar.

"It's going to be all right," I said, keeping my voice low and calm. She started to cry, and I put my arm around her. "Believe me, it will be OK. But we need to keep our heads. I need for you to stay strong, all right?"

"Yes."

"Let's go to my car. We can talk on the way."

I picked up her bag and managed to lug it down the aisle. Melanie followed me off. I looked around, blinking in the bright sunlight, trying to remember where I'd parked. Several rows from the building.

"I'll bring the car," I said. "I won't be long. OK?"

She nodded. I guessed she understood. She didn't look like she was going anywhere. I could be back with the car in no time.

As I jogged out into the lot, I realized that lifting her bag off the rack had aggravated my injuries. I was starting to feel a little tired, too. I backed my pace down to a quick walk, which still jolted my insides a little too much for comfort.

I heard it before I saw it. A car, one row away from me, moving fast, then screeching to a halt. It was the Lincoln.

My legs went wobbly, and I began to back away. One door opened, then another. A man unfolded himself from the car.

The man with the scarred face. He looked right at me. I turned and ran toward the bus.

I heard the doors slam and footsteps, as well as the rev of the Lincoln's engine as it took off. I was too scared to look behind me or notice the pain as my feet hit the pavement. My feet pounded out a bass line to the tune in my head—*escape, escape, escape, escape.* I came up on the bus and, without missing a beat, threw a hand up and caught the back end, propelling myself around the corner, heading toward the door, where Melanie still stood, looking at me, startled.

"Run!" I yelled.

"My bag."

"Fuck the bag! Run!" I grabbed her arm and yanked her into motion.

We ran into the cafeteria. I looked for the cops, but couldn't find them in the crowd. Where was the emergency exit? There had to be one somewhere.

"What are we doing?" Melanie said, sounding frantic. "We can't just stand here."

I glanced at the door. Any second, they could come in.

"Rest rooms," I said, pointing the way. We hurried to the ladies' and ducked inside.

As I took a momentary breather, Melanie said, "I hope you're not relying on that door to stop them."

I gave her a look. "I was sort of hoping there might be a window."

There was a window. It was a small rectangle of window, but big enough for us to wriggle through. It was also several feet out of reach.

Melanie looked exasperated. "We should have gone through the kitchen. It probably has a back door."

"I didn't see an easy way back there, did you? Besides, the staff would've seen us. I think the boys would've figured it out pretty fast."

"And they're not going to figure out we're in here?"

"Too late to worry about it now. Let's concentrate on getting out that window."

I looked around. Fortunately, the place still used freestanding trashcans, nice and big. I grabbed one and dragged it toward the window, ignoring the throbbing pain that coursed through my gut. Melanie saw my problem. She helped me get it there and turn it upside down, spilling trash everywhere. This drew a few curious looks from women banging in and out of the stalls, although oddly, no one bothered to ask what we were doing. I guess no one wanted to get involved with a couple of lunatics turning trashcans upside down in a bus stop bathroom. Imagine that.

Melanie helped me climb onto the container, which put me just high enough to grab the window frame.

"You're right," Melanie said. "This is a much more subtle approach." Despite her fear, she managed a smile.

I gave her a look, then snickered. "Yeah, well … I'll go through first. Can you give me a push?"

In agony, I hauled myself up and through the window as Melanie pushed from below. I was happy to see bare dirt and shrubs on the other side, and the drop wasn't all that bad. I wriggled through farther and turned myself over, planting my butt on the sill. Reaching back with one hand, I was able to grab a tall shrub. It was awkward and I thought I'd dislocate a shoulder in the process, but I was able to half-shimmy, half-pull myself through until my feet cleared the window and landed on the ground with a jarring thud.

"Jesus," I said, doubling over from the effort. "OK," I called to Melanie. After a moment, I saw her face in the window. I helped her through the process as best I could.

Looking out for the Lincoln and the two thugs, we did a fast zigzag through the lot, keeping low.

Melanie tugged my sleeve. "What about my bag?" she whispered.

"Let's find the car first."

I saw the Mustang in the distance. We ran to it, glancing around nervously, and got in.

I jammed the key in the ignition and turned it. The engine coughed. Then, nothing.

"Shit," I whispered.

"Oh, God." I looked at Melanie. She was staring down the row. Following her gaze, I saw Scarface running toward us.

"Shit, shit, shit." I turned the key again. The engine groaned and whined. Melanie whimpered. I banged the steering wheel. A stupid waste of time. I turned the key again. The engine started to respond, then died. Scarface was close now. He reached inside his jacket.

"Oh, no," Melanie said, sounding hysterical.

"C'mon, damn it," I yelled, stomping on the gas pedal as I tried again. The engine sputtered and roared. I slammed the car into drive forcing Scarface to lunge out of harm's way as I took off. Weaving slightly, I barreled down the row. It was a miracle I could drive at all. I was so frantic with fear, I could scarcely grip the wheel. Melanie wailed. My entire body shook. I gulped and kept going.

When I checked the rearview mirror, I realized the Lincoln was behind us, gaining speed. I took the next turn. Row upon row of cars. Where the hell was the exit? I looked back again. The Lincoln had just made the turn to follow us. Then, a tan car shot out from a row between us and the Lincoln. For some reason, the car stopped. The Lincoln was blocked.

I hit the gas and emerged into an empty area of the lot. The exit was a few hundred feet away. I headed straight for it, then to the interstate.

Chapter TEN

It was a long time before either of us spoke—probably only ten minutes, but it seemed longer.

Various parts of my body were talking to me, with nothing particularly good to say. If my doctor had seen me, I don't think he would have had anything good to say either.

Melanie looked almost catatonic. Now and then, I checked to see if she was still breathing.

Finally, she muttered something.

"What?" I asked.

"My luggage …"

I sighed. "I know. I'm hoping the bus driver or somebody noticed it. You can use my cell to call Greyhound if you want." I dug the little-used phone from my purse. I'd bought the thing only for emergencies. This seemed to qualify.

While Melanie tracked down the number and made the arrangements, I scanned signs for the next *food, gas, lodging* exit and pulled into the first place I saw, a Perkins Restaurant. As Melanie hung up, she said, "What are we doing here?"

"Getting something to eat. What do you think?"

"How can you think of food?"

"It could do you good. We've got a couple of hours to drive ahead of us."

Inside, we took a booth. The waitress came, and Melanie ordered toast, changing it to a club sandwich only after I insisted she get more. I decided to carbo-load on a big stack of pancakes, and we split a "Perkins Famous Bottomless Pot of Coffee."

Melanie's face was regaining its color, but she still looked rattled. I felt drained. I was tempted to order two pots of coffee.

"Do you think this is a good idea?" Melanie glanced out the window. "Those guys might still be looking for us."

"I doubt it. They're probably on their way back to Maryland, and they're not going to stop at every restaurant and gas station on the way to look for us."

We fell silent again. I tried to gauge when I could ask questions. I was also trying to figure out which ones to ask first.

"So," Melanie said after our coffee came. "Tom ... what happened?"

"He was shot. Found dead in Bruce Schaeffer's apartment."

"God." She shook her head. "And they think I did it? That's a good one."

"How's that?"

"Well, between the Mob and his so-called friends, there are plenty of other suspects."

"That may be," I said. "But you're the one who ran."

"I told you—"

"And I'm just telling you how it looks."

She said nothing for a moment, then nodded. "Pretty bad, I guess."

"Definitely not good." I paused. "So you didn't know Tom was dead?"

"No, I didn't. The last time I saw him, he was alive."

"When was that?"

"Saturday—the day after we met at your office. When I got home that night, I found a letter from Tom slid under my door. He apologized for everything he'd done. He said he understood it was over, but he had to talk to me about something, and it

70

couldn't be over the phone. He also said he was in danger. Maybe I was, too.

"I thought at first he was crazy. Or trying to provoke me. But something made me call him."

She paused looking at me. "He sounded strange. I could tell something was different about him right away. I asked why we couldn't talk on the phone, and he said some weird shit about wiretaps. It was nuts. I would've thought the whole thing was BS, if he hadn't sounded so … unlike himself, you know?"

I nodded. "Sure."

"We agreed to meet at his place the next day. I wanted to pick a coffee shop or something, but he didn't want to meet in public. That bothered me. I tried to change his mind, but he insisted.

"So I went there. He looked awful. He had grown a beard and lost weight. He told me that someone in the New York Mob was after him, and they might come after me, too."

"Did he say why?" I asked.

"He wasn't specific. Something about a conversation he recorded. He didn't spell it out, but I got the feeling he was blackmailing the guy."

"Not very bright."

"That's Tom—smart in some ways, clueless in others. He is—" She caught herself and frowned. "Was a very clever liar. He was bright, but had no judgment."

"So what did you do?"

"I still wasn't sure I was in danger. I believed he thought I was, but I didn't know what to do about it. I started thinking about what he said. For instance, I'd been getting phone calls— blocked calls—from someone who would hang up when I answered. Tom didn't do that. He'd always try to talk to me."

Our food came, but Melanie didn't seem interested. She had barely sipped her coffee, and I was on my second cup.

"You really should eat," I said.

She shrugged, then picked up a sandwich wedge and nibbled on one corner.

"What made you change your mind? About being in danger?"

"When I got home, one of my neighbors said someone had been asking about Tom and me. Someone with a New York accent, she said. She told him Tom moved out, but she didn't tell him anything else, even though he asked a lot of questions. She said he was a little scary. Kind of a big guy with a scar. No doubt that guy who chased us today. When he left, she saw him get into a big black car."

She put the sandwich down and stared at it. "That pretty much settled it for me. I decided to leave and get a motel room. I packed as much as I could into a bag and left. I figured I'd drive until I found something out of the way. While I was looking around, I noticed a black car that seemed to be following me. I freaked out. Lucky for me I happened to be near a state police barracks. When I pulled in, the car took off.

"I waited a while, then went back to my apartment and called a cab. I had the driver take me to the domestic violence center. I watched to make sure we weren't followed. They fixed me up in a shelter home. I told them Tom was violating the order. Technically, that was true, though it wasn't why I was seeking shelter. Anyhow, that's where I was for some time."

"There was no one you felt you could turn to?" I asked.

"I didn't want to put anyone else at risk," she said. "And I didn't want to go back to the motel, because it seemed too dangerous at that point. Someone could call and ask if I was registered. The shelter home locations are confidential. No one but the staff and the residents know where they are. I just needed to buy time. I knew I couldn't stay there forever."

"So you decided to leave town."

"Yes, a couple of days ago. I made the arrangements quickly." She looked at me. "Did Jenna tell you I was coming?"

I nodded. "She had your best interests at heart."

"I know. I'm glad she did, actually."

I wanted to believe that was true.

"Did Jenna tell you I called her?" I asked.

Melanie hesitated. "I don't recall her saying that."

"Really? Because she told me she mentioned it."

She shook her head. I couldn't think of any reason for Jenna to lie, but I could think of a few reasons Melanie might.

"Even so, why didn't you call me?" I asked.

"Why?" she said, looking disgusted. "So I could get a restraining order against the Mob?"

Good point. Even if Jenna told her to call me, maybe she didn't bother because it was futile. I couldn't argue with that. But now we were getting to the harder questions. "Did Tom ever mention someone named Gregory Knudsen?" I asked.

She shook her head.

"The FBI agent said he had something to do with the Mob guy."

"I've never heard of him."

I finished off my pancakes. Melanie managed to eat half a sandwich and had the rest boxed to go. I took care of the bill.

As we got in the car, I said, "If you don't know Gregory Knudsen, I'm assuming you also don't know about a certain post office box in College Park."

"Huh?"

"A post office box in my name."

"What are you talking about?"

"Did you go back to your place at any time after you went to the domestic violence center?"

"Are you kidding? Of course not."

I put the key in the ignition, then turned to face her, propping my arm on the back of the seat. "I need you to be very honest with me here."

"I have been honest with you."

"All right. Here it is. Someone pretending to be me tried to open a ten-thousand-dollar credit line in my name. Do you know anything about that? Because I found the paperwork in your apartment."

"What were you doing in my apartment?"

I told her about Donna's request, and how my attempt to find her had led me to the P.O. Box key.

Melanie looked stunned.

"When I went back to your place to return the key, there was a big box of files. Paperwork on my credit line and information on other people, too. Somebody's been committing identity theft in a major way. What do you know about it?"

"I … I don't know anything," she said.

I still wasn't sure whether to trust her. "Well, those papers were in your apartment. The cops have searched your place, so they probably have them now."

Melanie stared at me. "You think I tried to rip you off?"

I didn't know what to say, so I didn't say anything. I buckled up and turned the key in the ignition. This time, nothing happened. I tried again. The car was dead. I moaned in frustration and banged the wheel. Melanie continued to stare at me.

I sighed and reached for the cell phone again.

Chapter ELEVEN

I lay back on the bed with a groan, stared at the pebbled plaster ceiling of our motel room, and prayed for the day to end quickly.

Melanie sat cross-legged on the other bed, watching some show about young female lawyers in microminis and "fuck me" Manolo Blahniks, who couldn't understand why the senior partners at their firm weren't taking them seriously.

Sending the car off behind a tow truck left us little choice but to walk to a nearby motel. The price was right, and a woman at the front desk with a broad smile and a mole of unique proportions on her nose assured us the ice machine was probably working.

Sudlerville, Pennsylvania, was a small town with few diversions. It had an auto repair shop and a motel, both AAA-approved. It also had a shopping center, a church, a Moose Lodge, and an old movie theater that showed retrospective films on weekends. It was a place of stone houses built close together, tucked behind gnarly oaks, and no doubt owned by the sons and daughters of the sons and daughters of the sons and daughters of the city founders.

All I really cared about was that the bed was comfortable, the room was clean, and my car would be ready the next day.

Melanie yawned and stretched. She got up and walked to the dresser, where she'd put her leftover sandwich.

I wondered if the dresser had held anyone's clothes since its arrival at the motel.

"Now, I'm hungry," she said, returning to the bed with the box and plopping down. Those were the first words she'd spoken since we checked in.

"I think there's a McDonald's down the road, if you want more."

She thought about it. "Maybe. I almost feel too tired to bother, you know?"

On screen, one of the high-fashion lawyers was going to court with a thin file tucked under one arm and a determined pout on her collagen-enhanced lips.

I wondered if Melanie liked baseball. I didn't know if there was a game on. Would they watch the Orioles here or the Pittsburgh Pirates?

"I didn't try to steal from you."

I looked at Melanie. She kept her eyes on the tube.

"OK," I said.

"I don't know anything about identity theft or where those papers came from." She paused. "But Tom might have."

I rolled onto my side and perched my head on one hand. "Tom?"

"He was a computer expert, you know?"

"I didn't know. Who did he work for?"

"He had his own business. Computer consulting and web hosting. In fact, he did some work for the bank. That's how we met."

"I've read a little about those cases," I said. "There've been some big ones, where employees get personal data from their employers' databases and steal hundreds of thousands of dollars. A bank would be a great place to get that kind of data."

Melanie grimaced. "If he was making big money from identity theft, he never told me. He was always trying to *borrow* from me."

It seemed inconsistent, but there could have been an explanation. "Maybe he kept the money hidden, the way regular thieves will hide a stash until the heat's off, as they say in the movies."

"You'd still think he could have risked using a couple of hundred, now and then."

"True."

Melanie chewed her sandwich. In silence, we watched a commercial featuring a grinning woman who wore Depends and whose days were apparently spent in a nonstop series of tennis games and deck parties.

"Donna never mentioned that, about Tom working for the bank," I said. "Not that she'd have a reason. By the way, she's very concerned about you."

Melanie sighed. "Really? She got mad at me for a while about Tom. She thought it was dumb for me to start a relationship with a guy I hardly knew. Obviously, she was right. I had no idea about his problems. There's so much I still don't know about him."

What do we know about anyone? What did I know about Melanie? She was a client. Usually, I trust my instincts about people, and she had seemed OK when I first met her. Now a series of strange circumstances was challenging my first impression. Were the circumstances evidence of the truth or a muddling of the truth?

"You know, I think I will walk over to that McDonald's," I said. "I can bring back something if you like."

"OK. Maybe one of those salads? With ranch dressing?" She retrieved her purse. "This should cover it. Hey, incidentally ..."

"Yeah?"

"I never properly thanked you. I wasn't sure I should go back at first, but I think you're right. I can't run from this." She looked directly at me. "And I am innocent."

I nodded, still not sure.

φ φ φ

On the way to McDonald's, I called directory assistance for Donna's home number and rang her up. I wondered how much the long-distance would cost me. I couldn't even remember if it was included in my plan.

Donna sounded distracted, but relieved. "Where was she?"

"On her way out of town," I said, keeping it vague. Maybe I was paranoid, but somehow it seemed safer for everyone if I kept our location a secret. "We're heading back."

"Out of town? Where?"

"Not far. I'll tell you later. You wouldn't believe what's been going on. The important thing is, Melanie's fine."

"Good. Thanks, Sam."

"Something wrong?"

"Hmm. No, no. It's been difficult for me, that's all."

"While I'm at it, I want to check something out with you," I said. "Melanie says Tom did some work for the bank."

There was a pause. "Well, yes."

"Working on the computers?"

"Right."

"How long ago was that?"

"Several months."

"Have you had any security breaches since then?"

A longer pause. "Not that I know of. Why?"

"Just wondering."

"There must be some reason you're interested."

"No, nothing in particular. I'd better go. I'll be in touch sometime after we get back."

"Sam, there's something—" She stopped.

"What?"

"Never mind. I'll talk to you later."

I shrugged and disconnected.

At McDonald's, I got a salad for Melanie, a Filet-O-Fish for myself. There was little traffic as I walked back to the motel. The sun had already set in a rosy glow. The twilight was warm and pleasant, a little less humid than at home. Off in the woods, away from the road, I saw swarms of fireflies, emitting brief flashes of phosphorescent light in upward strokes. A lone bird peeped at intervals.

I thought about Melanie's explanation. She could have been right about Tom. I had an account at First Bank of Laurel. If that box of files was any indication, I was one victim among many.

The motel lot had few cars. From what I could see, only two other rooms had guests. I wondered how the place stayed in business.

One car seemed familiar, but I couldn't think where I'd seen it. It was nondescript, a light color. Like about a million other cars. But this one ... what was it? I knew I'd seen it before, but couldn't remember where.

Melanie met me at the door, and we divvied up the food. As we ate, the image of the car continued to nag at me. Then I realized ... it could have been the car that cut off the Lincoln back in Breezewood.

I didn't want to alarm Melanie, but I did want to check it out. "Hey, I didn't get drinks," I said. "You want a soda?"

"OK. Anything without caffeine."

I went outside and took a stroll by the car, keeping a distance, trying not to be obvious. It was tan, like the one in Breezewood. It was also an older model—maybe twenty years, maybe older. One of those boxy jobs with a lot of power. I still wasn't sure it was the same car, but the resemblance was close.

I shook my head. *You're paranoid.* That's what I thought when I saw the Lincoln. Of course, if it was the same car, the driver had done us a favor. What do you call it when you think you're being stalked by friends, rather than enemies?

I found the soda machine and got a couple of ginger ales. On the way back, I slowed to look at the car again. A Ford Fairlane. Lots of power, no style.

I guess I was tired. I didn't hear him approach. He was only a few feet away when he said, "Not as old as yours, but a classic in its own way."

I whirled around. He stood there, looking at me with that same shit-eating grin he'd had in my office.

"John Drake, I presume," I said, trying to ignore the way my heart was pounding in my chest.

His smile broadened. "I guess you saw through that one." He wore a light sports jacket and a pair of slacks. Why so dressed up, here in the middle of Nowheresville P-A on a warm summer night?

"Who the hell are you and what are you doing here?"

"I'm an interested friend. And it's a good thing I'm here, or you might not be."

"I suppose so," I said. "I take it I have you to thank for getting out of Breezewood without the Mob on my tail."

"Stavos would probably have caught up with you. Your car isn't in the best shape."

"I'm afraid it's the only one I have. But let's get back to you. See, I know who Stavos is and why he's following me. You, on the other hand, I haven't a clue about."

"Sam?" Melanie had come outside. She walked up to us. "What's going on?"

"Are you Melanie Hayes?" the stranger said.

She looked at me, then at him. "Yes."

He reached inside his jacket.

"Melanie, run!" I yelled.

Melanie's eyes widened. She started to turn. Meanwhile, the man had already seized her shoulder with his free hand. I tried to grab his other arm, but he pulled it away. His hand emerged from beneath the jacket—holding an envelope.

"My name is Reed Duvall, Ms. Hayes. I'm a private investigator." He handed her the envelope. "And you've just been served."

Chapter TWELVE

I finished reading the complaint for the second time. Melanie had fallen, face down, on the bed and hadn't moved since we returned to the room.

"It's thorough," I said.

Melanie lifted her head from the pillow and looked at me with disgust. "Wonderful. Any more good news?"

"Sorry." I set the complaint aside. "I know this must be hard, but try not to worry. It's really the bank they're after. Of course …"

"What?"

"The bank's liability depends pretty much on you."

She groaned. "Well, I never did anything."

According to the complaint, the plaintiff, a businessman trying to buy property in Prince George's County was unable to do so because someone, without his knowledge, borrowed twenty thousand dollars in his name—twenty thousand that was never paid back. Allegedly, that person was Melanie Hayes who, either with or without Tom Garvey's help, got his personal information through her job at First Bank of Laurel. The businessman believed this because the paperwork for the twenty-thousand-dollar loan was discovered, along with similar paperwork for other First Bank of Laurel depositors, in Melanie Hayes' apartment.

The 30-page complaint threw every claim in the book against the bank, its officers, and anyone with any potential responsibility on down the line to Melanie. Donna was a defendant, too.

No wonder Donna seemed nervous when I asked her about a possible breach of security at the bank. Her job was probably on the line.

My friend, Jamila Williams, signed the complaint. I didn't know she handled litigation.

"If they're after the bank, why am I being sued?" Melanie asked.

"It's standard procedure to name every possible defendant. Like I said, the whole case depends on you, unless they dig up other evidence. The bank will probably argue that you were acting outside the scope of your employment or violating their policy. In other words, they weren't responsible. If the court agrees, that leaves you—"

"Holding the bag."

"Yeah."

Melanie put her head in her hands. "I'm going crazy. The whole world is going crazy." She pushed herself upright and faced me, her legs crossed Indian-style. "Look," she said, rubbing the bridge of her nose with both hands. "So they sued me. Let's say they win. I don't have what they're looking for. I don't have any money at all."

I nodded. "It's the bank that's got the deep pockets here. They can get a judgment, but collecting on it is a whole 'nother thing. You don't own real estate, do you?"

"Real estate? Ha. I have a ten-year-old car and about eight hundred dollars in savings. Not a lot to show, after 36 years on earth, huh?"

I shrugged. "My car's older, and my savings account isn't much more impressive."

Melanie laughed. "We make quite a pair." She looked away, as if sorry she'd said that. "I don't mean to presume anything. I'd like to hire you for this, if that's OK."

"I guess it's OK," I said, slowly, thinking aloud. "I was lucky enough to avoid a problem, even though my information got out somehow. Of course, the bank's legal counsel may offer to represent you ... but, under the circumstances, you may want to get separate counsel—"

"Will you help me?" She blurted.

I paused. I was starting to believe Melanie was set up. Why would she keep all those records? And her story about leaving Maryland made sense.

"All right. But if something comes up—a conflict of interest—you may need to change attorneys."

She looked resigned. "OK."

"Is there anything else you can tell me about this?"

She lifted her hand and dropped it. "I've already told you everything I know."

"No thoughts on who might have put those papers in your apartment?"

"Tom?"

"They weren't there when I first went to your place, and Tom was dead long before that. Anyone else?"

"Maybe it was Bruce."

"That reminds me. He called you a couple of times last week."

"Bruce? I wonder why."

"I wondered the same thing. I spoke to him, when I was looking for you. Based on what he said, he didn't strike me as a close friend."

Melanie snorted. "He's not. He probably thinks I killed Tom."

"For all we know, he could have killed Tom."

"When I last saw Tom, he said Bruce had gone away for the weekend."

"Maybe Bruce arranged for someone else to kill him. Anyway, I think it's interesting that both times I went to your apartment, I found evidence that could be used against you on the identity theft charge, and I saw Bruce's number on your caller ID."

Her eyebrows drew together. "You think maybe he was calling to make sure no one was home, and he put the stuff there?" She shrugged. "He has no reason to talk to me. Sometimes, I get the feeling he might actually be jealous of me. Not in any sexual sense. It's just that Bruce and Tom were so tight. More than friends. Bruce used to help Tom out with his business. Financial stuff, marketing."

"Does Bruce work on computers, too?"

"No, that was strictly Tom's thing. Bruce manages a club or lounge of some sort. He lined up a project for Tom at the club and worked closely with him, setting up the system. He knows people, too.

"Tom had just moved to the area when I met him, and he told me Bruce was helping him make local contacts. I know how hard that can be. I've moved around a lot myself. Anyhow, Bruce hooked Tom up with the club's owner. Real rich guy with a lot of businesses. Has an amazing house on Gibson Island. We went there once for a party."

"Can you remember his name?"

"Conrad Ash. He goes by Connie."

"When I was in your apartment, I found a bar napkin with the name Connie and a phone number written on it. I assumed it was a woman."

She smiled. "I can't swear to it, but I think it was probably Connie Ash. He called Tom about various projects, until things started to fall apart. I think the same thing that wrecked our relationship affected his work. They had a big argument at one point, and I think Connie stopped using him after that. Even so, Bruce and Tom kept meeting at the club. They tried to be secretive about it, but it was easy to tell." She tapped her nose. "Tom would come home, smelling like a smokehouse."

"What did they do there?"

"Tom said they were working, but never said on what." She arched an eyebrow. "I wondered if he was gambling or doing drugs because of all his debts. Or if there was another woman."

Melanie fell silent for a moment, then drew her knees up and hugged them. "So, after we go to the police … what happens?"

"They'll book you, fingerprint you, and put you in a holding cell. At some point, they'll question you. There's a federal agent involved, and he may want to question you separately."

"Will they want to hold me before the trial?"

"I'll try to get you out on your own recognizance, but they may seek bail. You did leave the state, but I can argue you didn't know what was going on. Hopefully, I can work something out with the prosecutor."

She brushed her hair back from her face with one hand, looking distracted. "I have to tell you, I'm scared."

I tried to be reassuring, but I couldn't blame her. "They may keep you for one night, but like I said, there are factors weighing in your favor here. You have friends, a job."

"Do I?" She grimaced, and tears formed in the corners of her eyes. "I've probably lost my job. The only person who knows me well is Donna. I don't know where I stand with her right now."

I thought about my phone call to her. "She's probably in a difficult position."

"I know. I screwed up again. She's done so much for me, and look where it's gotten her." She wiped the tears away fiercely, before they could reach her cheeks. "Look where it's gotten me. I deserve everything I get."

"Don't say that." The words came out like an order.

She looked at me, surprised.

"Don't stop believing in yourself," I said, more softly. "You can't."

When worse comes to worse, that's all you have, I thought. When the whole world stops believing you, who else is there? Maybe the bank would try to leave Melanie twisting in the wind.

Maybe Donna would disavow all knowledge of Melanie's actions, to paraphrase the old *Mission Impossible* refrain. If it was going to get ugly, it was up to me to tell Melanie not to lose faith. Sometimes being an attorney is like that. It's more than legal analysis—it's like being a shrink, a priest, a spokesperson, and a lifestyle consultant, all in one.

I looked out the window. In the dark, I could see Duvall's car. After doing his job, he'd beat a hasty retreat to his room.

"I'm going to talk to that process server," I said, looking at her. "You all right?"

"Sure." Melanie's voice was little more than a whisper. "Thanks, Sam."

I touched her arm. "We all make mistakes. You wouldn't believe the ones I've made."

Melanie looked at me, red-eyed, but smiling.

"That's more like it." I retrieved my pen and notebook from my purse. "Be right back."

I stepped into the warm night, walked to Duvall's room, and knocked on the door. The window curtain moved, and a few seconds later, he opened the door.

"How's my guardian angel?" I asked.

"Doing fine. To what do I owe the pleasure of this visit?"

"It's more business than pleasure."

He gave me a mock look of disappointment. "Well, come in."

Since this wasn't the Hilton or even Motel 6, the rooms were sparsely furnished. Duvall sat on the edge of the only bed. I opted for leaning against the dresser.

"You never told us how you knew where we were," I said.

"It's called surveillance. I knew you were looking for Melanie, so I kept tabs on you."

"How did you know I was looking for Melanie?"

"Connections."

"If you had me under surveillance, where were you last week when Stavos and his guys decided to beat the crap out of me?"

"I had to get client approval for the surveillance since it was going to require so much time." He looked at me with regret. "By the time I started, you'd landed in the hospital. You look like you're in pretty good shape now, considering."

"I'm all right. Can I ask you something?"

"Shoot. Can't guarantee you I'll answer."

"Fair enough. Can you tell me whether you've served the other defendants?"

"Sure. Your client was the last one. It's tough to serve someone who doesn't want to be found."

I nodded. So Donna knew about the case when I spoke to her.

"Are you still working on this?" I said. "Or is your job pretty much done?"

"I was hired to investigate who was responsible for the client's debt," Duvall said. "Based on what I found, Ms. Williams drew up the complaint and had me serve the defendants. Whether she'll have more work for me after this, I don't know."

"That connection who told you I was looking for Melanie. Someone with the police?"

Duvall looked at me.

"OK," I said. "I figured I'd ask."

"We all have to do our jobs."

"Yes, you certainly did yours, Mr. *Drake*."

He gave me his white, even-toothed smile. "It was creative, you must admit."

"Do you always go around pretending to be someone else?"

"Only if I think someone might recognize me. I mentioned to Ms. Williams that I was going to see you, and she said my name had come up in a recent conversation."

"You could have been straight with me."

"How could I know you would cooperate?"

"I didn't cooperate anyway."

He shrugged. "That's the way it crumbles sometimes. Tell me, Ms. McRae, do you always go around browbeating people?"

"Who's browbeating? We're just making conversation."

"About a case. With someone who works for the opposing attorney."

"No rule against that," I said. "I can talk to you. It's Jamila's client and *his* employees or agents that are off-limits."

"Such fine distinctions."

"Important ones."

"I love listening to attorneys talk about so-called legal ethics," he said, crossing his arms and leaning back. "It's interesting to imagine *legal* and *ethics* in the same sentence, let alone as a phrase."

"Almost as interesting as imagining a private detective invoking high moral ground."

"Ouch. You wound me, madam."

"Imagine how I feel."

"Shall we call it a draw and leave it at that?"

"It's a draw then," I said. I got up and walked to the door, then turned to him. "But I suspect I won't be able to leave it at that."

He grinned. "I certainly hope not."

Chapter THIRTEEN

We bailed my car out of the garage and checked out of the motel the next morning at around ten. Duvall had already left. The ride home felt longer than it was, but the car was running. It had only cost me several hundred dollars in repairs, a night's stay at a cheap motel, and ten years off my life from the close call in Breezewood. I'd have to remember to put preventive maintenance a little higher on my to-do list.

Melanie was quiet. She looked like I was taking her to her execution. I turned on the radio to fill the uncomfortable silence. After stopping for lunch, we went to the police.

I waited up front while they processed her. Detective Derry came out and motioned me to follow him. He took me down a hall, past a series of offices to a conference room where they seemed to be holding a convention of suits. One of them was Jergins. The rest I'd never seen before.

"This is Ms. Hayes' attorney, Sam McRae," Derry said to the group sitting around a long table. "Why don't you introduce yourselves? You already know Special Agent Jergins."

Jergins gave me a terse nod. A woman next to him with red poodle-cut hair said she was Special Agent Simmons with the FBI's Baltimore field office. Assistant Director Trask came next—a gray-haired man whose mouth turned down in a look of faint disapproval or worry. He was also from Baltimore. A special agent from the Bureau's DC headquarters mumbled his name without looking up from the papers he was reading. I couldn't believe the manpower the feds were putting into this one. You'd think these guys were after Dillinger.

There was an empty chair between the FBI contingent and two other people, a man and woman.

"Special Agent Joe Petrocelli, ma'am," the man said in a booming voice. He had a swarthy complexion, a dark buzz cut, and a nose shaped like a pepper.

"Special Agent Marla Holmes." The woman was about ten years younger, with brown hair, green eyes, and freckles that made her look like she ought to be in an Irish Spring commercial.

"And which part of the FBI are you with?" I said.

"Not FBI, ma'am," Petrocelli said. "Secret Service."

"Secret Service?"

"Yes, ma'am. We have jurisdiction over major identity theft cases."

"The Bureau, of course, will also be investigating this matter," the mumbling agent from DC said.

"Secret Service has *primary* jurisdiction," Petrocelli said. I looked at Agent Holmes. She could have been playing poker in the Irish Spring commercial.

"Your jurisdiction is *concurrent* with ours over federally insured financial institutions," the red-haired poodle-cut said.

"I'm sure my counterpart at Treasury will be happy to cooperate with the Bureau on this," the gray-haired Trask said, his brow furrowed with parallel lines. "Of course, as assistant director, I'll be coordinating your efforts on this case."

"With all due respect, assistant director," Petrocelli said, making an authoritative if meaningless gesture with one hand, "our superiors at Treasury may not agree to share jurisdiction over certain aspects of this matter."

"I don't think they'll have much choice." It was Jergins. Always the diplomat.

I looked at Derry. His eyes were closed. Perhaps he was thinking about early retirement.

"Excuse me," I said. Everyone looked at me. "Are we going to talk about my client? What are the charges? Do you intend to question her and when?"

"We'll get to that in a moment, ma'am," Petrocelli said. I wished he would stop calling me that. "We need to work out the logistics. I still think we should question Ms. Hayes as a group."

"And I still think we should question her separately," Ms. Poodle Cut said.

Derry spoke. "The decision's been made." He opened his eyes. "We'll question her in shifts. Agent Jergins will go first. Agent Simmons will follow. Then the Secret Service. I'll sit in on all sessions."

Trask, the assistant director, leaned forward. "That wasn't my—"

Derry cut him off with a look that would have stopped a speeding freight train. "Meanwhile," Derry continued, "I'll talk to Ms. Hayes myself."

"Are we sure we want to proceed just yet?" the DC mumbler said. "Isn't the Maryland AG interested? What about DOJ? Or the FTC?"

"Or the SPCA?" I asked. Everyone looked at me as if I'd passed gas, except Agent Holmes, who continued to play poker.

"Unlike the federal government, we can't drag things out forever," Derry said, giving Mumbles a pointed look. "Get your act together and let me know when you're ready to see her client." He turned to me and said, "Let's go."

Derry strode down the hall with me double-timing beside him. "Sorry about that. This was, supposedly, decided."

"Quite a crew in there."

"Too damned many cooks." He reddened a little. It was the first time I'd heard him swear.

"You don't need them to go forward with your own charges."

"Sure, but I'm getting pressure from above to cooperate with them. I'd like to see the chief handle these … people."

I got the feeling he might have chosen a word other than people if I'd been a fellow cop. Or a man. "Hard to coordinate," I said.

He shook his head. "It'll get done. Meanwhile, let's take care of business. Your client's looking at possible identity theft and murder charges."

"The identity theft charge is iffy at best."

"We have what we have. She worked at the bank. She and Garvey could have worked together."

"Tom Garvey was a computer expert. He could have accessed those records himself."

"Or maybe she helped him. When she kicked him out, maybe he threatened to tell on her. Maybe she killed him to protect herself."

"And maybe I'll win a million bucks in the next Lotto. You're grasping at straws. Who says there's a connection between the crimes? Besides, wouldn't Garvey also have been implicated?"

Derry shrugged. "So maybe he thought he could cut a deal. I don't know."

"Far as the murder goes, aren't there other suspects? What about the roommate? For that matter, the Mob guy could have done it."

"The Mob wouldn't leave a body lying around. As for the roommate—" He shrugged. "So far, we have nothing to go on."

"So he hasn't been ruled out?"

Derry didn't say anything. As far as I was concerned, that meant yes.

"Have you found the gun yet?" I asked.

He shook his head.

We stopped at the door to the interrogation room. Through a window, I could see Melanie, hunched in a chair, staring at her clenched hands.

"Can you at least tell me what kind of gun?"

"Nine millimeter," he said, enunciating slowly and with exaggerated patience.

"So she goes there and shoots him and is careless enough to leave fingerprints, but cautious enough to get rid of the gun?"

Derry gave me the kind of look one might give a pesky child. "Perhaps I'll ask her," he said, in a quiet voice. He opened the door, and we stepped inside.

φ φ φ

After Derry questioned Melanie, I insisted on a break. Then Jergins took his turn. Mostly, he asked Melanie what she knew about Christof Stavos and Gregory Knudsen and the CD, which was nothing. I suggested we continue the questioning the next day.

I needed the postponement almost as badly as Melanie. She looked worn out, and I still felt the pain of physical recovery. My two-week "vacation" from work was turning into a busman's holiday.

The good news was that everything Melanie said was squaring with what she'd told me. The bad news was that Derry didn't appear to believe her.

"I think your case is a little light on evidence," I said. "You have no gun. On the identity theft charges, there's nothing other than that box of files."

"The neighbor swears he saw her on the scene."

"Did he hear the gunshots?"

"No. Said he was in the shower or something."

"How convenient. What about the identity theft charges? A box of files doesn't prove a thing."

Derry didn't say anything.

"Fine." I checked my watch. "God, it's late. Everyone at the state's attorney's office will have left by now."

"He's here."

I did a double take. "What?"

"Yeah. I was just talking to him."

"You're telling me the state's attorney assigned to this case is actually here?"

Derry shrugged. "This is big. Said he wanted to talk to you, too. I told him you might be a while. He's waiting up front."

I headed toward the lobby. State's attorneys usually confine themselves to their offices and the courtroom. The case must be big if this guy came all the way to the police station to discuss it with defense counsel—after hours no less.

I opened the door. Across the room, standing up to greet me, was Ray Mardovich.

Chapter FOURTEEN

"Hi," Ray said.

"Hi."

He smiled. "This is odd."

"Yeah."

I hadn't had a case with Ray recently. Ray worked the Circuit Court, handling jury trials on the murders, rapes, and major drug offenses that arose with great frequency in our county. My criminal cases rarely went to trial. When they did, the matters usually involved clients with exaggerated notions of their driving ability after 10 beers. Or people who believed in the socialist principle of the even distribution of wealth and expressed their support by redistributing other people's goods to themselves.

The fact that Ray was prosecuting was yet another sign that this case was serious.

"So?" I asked.

"So." He looked away for a moment.

I glanced at my scuffed shoes. "We can handle this, right?"

He nodded vigorously. "Sure."

"OK." I paused to gather my thoughts. Part of me wanted to kiss him. I was also aware of the pain I felt when I tried to reach him after my release from the hospital.

"I thought you were in San Diego," I said, trying to keep my voice neutral.

"San Francisco."

"Right."

"I got back yesterday."

"Was it nice?"

"Yeah. It's a beautiful city."

"It must be fun to travel. I never have the time or the money. Of course, I'm not wild about planes. You always hear about them falling out of the sky and people losing their luggage and all."

He looked at me warily. "What's wrong?"

"Nothing." I forced myself to look him in the eye. "Why don't we talk about the case?"

"Dinner first?"

"Oh, I don't know," I said. "I'm really tired and it's been a long day. I'm still—" I started to say that I was still sore from the beating, but I stopped myself. I wanted to tell him, but I didn't want to. I didn't want to get sucked into dinner. I didn't want to tell my problems to Ray. I couldn't depend on him.

"Still what?" he asked.

"Still tired from my drive. I drove to Pennsylvania and back."

"Yes, I heard."

"So I probably won't be very good company. And it's late. You probably want to get home."

"Helen won't mind," he said, giving me a meaningful look. "She's still in San Francisco."

So it was more than dinner I was being sucked into. It was another perfect opportunity. I wanted it, too. But a little voice said no. "My head. I'm just not feeling so hot. I'm sorry."

He nodded. "It's OK. We'll have other times."

"Let's get back to the case. The bail hearing—where are you on that? I assume you won't be asking too high an amount."

Ray hesitated. "I ... I'm not sure about that."

"What do you mean? We're talking about an employed, middle-class individual with a job, and community contacts. She should be released on her own recognizance."

"You can forget about an OR release. We're talking about a woman accused of murder and major fraud, big enough for the feds to take an interest. She also fled the jurisdiction."

"She didn't know about any of this," I said. "She left because she was afraid."

"Maybe. Maybe not."

"So what are you saying?"

"I'm leaning toward contesting any pretrial release. At best, we'll be asking for a very high bail, possibly as high as a hundred thousand."

I stared at him. "You must be joking."

"Sam, this is serious business—"

"Don't be condescending, Ray. Of course, it's serious, but my client doesn't have property. She's a university student who works at a bank. She's not a flight risk."

"She's got a spotty employment history. She also has a record in another state."

"What?" That stopped me cold. A background check is something I do as a matter of course for any criminal client. In this case, I hadn't had time.

"It's true," he said. "I've got the paperwork. She was picked up in Florida for shoplifting."

"How could she get a job at a bank with a record?"

"That's what I'd like to know. She got Florida's version of a stet, so maybe they missed it on the background check."

A "stet" is a case that gets continued and never goes to court, eventually getting dismissed. It was something short of probation—used frequently for first-time offenders.

"When was this?"

"A while ago."

"What does that mean, a while ago?"

"I don't know, maybe 15 years."

"So she was young and stupid. And she hasn't done anything since."

"I have my marching orders," he said. "You've got your arguments. Take your best shot."

"Ray, why can't we work something out?"

"This is a big case. I don't have a lot of room to move."

"My client is not one of those lowlifes you run across all the time in your cases."

He did a double take. "Oh? So, because your client isn't poor and black, she should get a free ticket out of the slammer?"

"That's not what I'm saying and you know it. There's no reason to be inflexible on this."

"You don't appreciate what I'm dealing with." He glared at me. "I've got three sets of cops telling me what's what, and my own boss is walking on eggshells to keep everyone happy. This is hot stuff."

"Maybe you should recuse yourself?"

He laughed. "On what grounds? Certainly, we're not going to bring up certain, uh, things we've done recently?"

"Of course not." I waved the thought away in irritation. "I don't know. There must be something."

"I'm sorry, but even if there were grounds, this case is dynamite. This is a real step up for me."

"What do you care?" I shot him an accusing look. "I thought you wanted to leave the state's attorney."

"Well, sure," he said. "But not right away."

"Face it, Ray, you're not going anywhere." My words flowed, fast and furious. "You're not leaving the state's attorney. You're not leaving—" I managed to stop myself in time. My hand felt cramped. I realized I was clutching a pen. It was a miracle it hadn't snapped in half.

"What are you talking about?"

"I'm talking about your job. You're not leaving the safety of your job." I wasn't talking about that. From the look on his face, he knew it. I squeezed my temples with one hand, trying to work out the tension. "This has been a rough few days," I said.

"I know."

"I'm sorry. I didn't mean to lose my temper."

He nodded.

"I guess we'll just have to play this out in court."

Ray gestured toward the door. "I've got some stuff for you in the car. Paperwork ..."

"OK."

We walked out together. He handed me the information.

"I'm sorry, too," he said.

"It's your job."

"Right."

"OK then. See you tomorrow."

"See you."

For a moment, we looked at each other. Any other time, we might have embraced. Not this time.

I walked away, willing myself not to look back. The sound of his car door slamming was like that of the lid closing on a casket.

Chapter FIFTEEN

The next day, Melanie's bail was set at fifty thousand dollars.

The feds continued their questioning marathon. During a break, I checked my messages. Donna had called to ask how things were going. I called her back.

I gave my name to whoever answered the phone. After a pause, Donna came on.

"Talk to me, Sam," she said.

"Her bail is fifty grand."

I heard a quick intake of breath at the other end.

"A bail bondsman will cost ten percent up front," I said.

"I've got it."

"You're going to pay the bondsman?"

"I have the money."

"That's nice," I said, for lack of anything better. The lawsuit against the bank was in the back of my mind. The case was already about as crazy as a quacking cow. Now a codefendant in a related case was bailing out my client.

As if she'd read my mind, Donna said, "I assume you know the bank's been sued."

"Yes, we know."

"We're both on unpaid leave until things are worked out. We could lose our jobs." She heaved a sigh. "For what it's worth, I don't think Melanie was involved. How's she doing, by the way?"

"Not bad, all things considered. How soon can you get here?" I wanted to get Melanie out as quickly as possible. There were too many cops and complications to waste time.

"I can leave right now."

"I appreciate what you're doing. I'm sure Melanie will, too."

"Believe me, Sam, I want to do this," she said. Her voice sounded strained. "I don't want her to be hurt."

I didn't say anything. I wondered if hurt might be unavoidable.

φ φ φ

Donna hung around until Melanie's release. The two hugged.

"I was thinking," Donna said to Melanie, "You'll need a place to stay."

"Your apartment is a mess," I said.

Melanie nodded. "I'm scared to go there anyway."

"I realize it might not be ... a good idea to stay with me," Donna said. "I was thinking I could pay for a motel, for a couple of days, until you can arrange something."

"I don't want to be a burden," Melanie said, her eyes downcast.

"It's not a burden, really."

"I'll take care of it."

"I don't mind—"

"No," Melanie said. "I'll do it."

"OK." Donna tried to catch Melanie's eye. Melanie kept looking at the floor. "Will you tell your parents?"

Melanie shrugged.

"Well," Donna said. "I can't tell you what to do."

"Greyhound still has your clothes," I said to Melanie. "I can give you a ride."

"Thanks."

After a round of awkward good byes, I drove Melanie to the Silver Spring Greyhound bus depot to pick up her bag. It was a coin toss, as far as whether my office or apartment was safer. I chose my apartment, only because I wouldn't have to answer Sheila's well-intentioned, but probing, questions.

Melanie flipped through the motel section of my Yellow Pages. I got on the computer and searched online.

"How many days you figure?" I asked.

"Just one night. Maybe two," she said. "Maybe I can set something up with a friend after that. Motels cost bucks."

"Why didn't you take Donna up on her offer?"

She shook her head. "I have to stop depending on her and other people. She's done too much already, getting me my job, sticking up for me when I wasn't around. I have to take some responsibility here."

"Which reminds me, you never mentioned your previous arrest."

Melanie looked up from the book. "That thing in Florida. Jeez ... I'd forgotten."

"You forgot you were arrested?"

"It was a long time ago. They dropped the charges."

"So Donna must have pulled some strings—so you could get your job."

"Yeah, she did." Melanie sighed. "Jesus, she must hate me."

"Anything but." I scrolled through a list of places. Everything was expensive.

"She gets me a job, and I get her fired," Melanie said.

"Hey, if she hated you, she wouldn't have sprung for your bail."

"She shouldn't have. It's 'cause of my parents, you know."

"Speaking of which, maybe you should call them." I shook my head. "I don't care what they say, these motels aren't cheap. We should just drive to the nearest Motel 6 or something."

"Sam, what do your parents think about your career?"

"Huh?" The change in topic threw me.

"I'm sorry. I shouldn't ask such a personal question."

"It's OK. Actually, my parents died when I was young."

"How old were you?"

"Nine."

"How awful."

"Well—" I shrugged. What was I supposed to say?

"My parents have never approved of my choices." Melanie sniffed. "They had it all worked out for me. I'd go to the right private college, meet some bright young man with a future, get married, and proceed to waste my overpriced education on a life of volunteer work and entertaining my husband's business associates. Ha. Thank God I didn't fall into that trap, huh? I would have missed out on all this fun."

I leaned my chair back. "So why not call them?"

Melanie's smile vanished. "Because they said if I didn't do what they wanted, they'd disown me. So I walked away. And I've never looked back."

Neither of us spoke for a while.

"Maybe things have changed," I said.

She shook her head. "Donna keeps in touch. When she told them I was going to the University of Maryland—" She looked away, her face reddening. "They didn't … they said they didn't care." She thrust a hand to her chest, which heaved with anger. "I took the initiative. I applied for college. I'm paying for it. And they don't care." She paused. "Screw them."

"So Donna—"

"Donna … God, she's like a mother to me." Melanie took a deep breath. "She's really something. But I have to show her I can stand on my own."

She looked at me. "You are amazing. I wish I had my act together like you."

I resisted the urge to burst out laughing. "Don't kid yourself. My act isn't all that together."

"But you didn't even have parents and look at you. A lawyer with your own business. That's something."

I guessed that it was. I also had a married boyfriend. I had a never-ending parade of bills and a constant struggle to keep up with them.

We left the apartment and cruised Route 1, until we found a decent-looking budget motel within walking distance of restaurants. Getting out, she said, "Wait a minute. What about you?"

"What about me?"

"Aren't they after you, too?"

That had occurred to me. "Maybe it would be a good idea to get a room here. The rates are good."

"We could share again."

I balked. I didn't want to offend Melanie, but I crave privacy. "Actually, I'm thinking about running by the club tonight. Check up on what Schaeffer and Garvey did there. I may stay late, and I don't want to wake you."

She shrugged. "OK."

I felt bad. Sharing would save her—and me—some bucks. But, at the end of the day, I just feel most relaxed when I'm alone, free of the need to make nice—even with a significant other.

We got adjoining rooms in back so my purple car wouldn't be on display. I left Melanie and ran by the office to pick up some stuff. I managed to sneak by Sheila's desk without questions or a lecture. Jamila had called. I wanted to talk to her anyway, so I returned the call while it was fresh in mind. She was stunned to discover that Melanie was my client.

"Well," she said. "It's a small world after all, huh?"

"Not only that," I said, "but she's the client who disappeared."

"The one whose ex-boyfriend was murdered?"

"The same."

"Man." Jamila sounded incredulous. "You can really pick 'em, huh?"

"Yeah, I have a knack for it. And, by the way, since when do you handle litigation?"

She sighed. "I don't. I hate it, but I got stuck with this thing, because I was the only one who knew the case and no one else would touch it."

"That much of a dog?"

"Not really. Everyone's throwing up their hands and saying, 'I don't know anything about this area of the law.' Well, who does? No one's an expert on identity theft law."

"By the way, remember that ten grand someone tried to borrow in my name? It's probably connected to your case. I have accounts at First Bank."

"Really?" she said. "This gets more interesting all the time. So are you dropping the client?"

"Well, no," I said, drawing the word out. "She's still my client. There's no conflict of interest here. I haven't lost any money because of the information leak." At least, I didn't think so. I was still waiting for my credit report.

For a moment, she was silent. "Are you serious?"

"Yes."

"She's still your client. Even though she may have tried to steal from you?"

"I don't think so."

"But you're not sure."

"I'm pretty sure."

"Why?"

"The circumstances aren't right. I was in her apartment after she disappeared and that box wasn't there. I came back later and the box was there. I think someone set her up."

"How do you know she didn't put the box there?"

"It's complicated," I said. I gave her the *CliffsNotes* version of the last few days' events. "She disappeared because she was scared. I don't think she would have come back to the apartment under those circumstances, certainly not to place incriminating evidence in plain view in her apartment. I can't prove she didn't do it, but I don't think she did."

"And you left her at a motel? Shouldn't you keep her with you?"

"I have a room there, too, but I can't be her babysitter. As long as she stays out of sight, I think she'll probably be OK."

"You don't think she'll run?"

"I don't think so. I really think she was desperate."

"Hmmm." Jamila sounded unconvinced.

"Have you spoken to the bank's counsel?" I asked.

"Yeah. They think they can get kicked from the case. They're claiming no responsibility for your client's actions."

I knew it. Shit. "My client has no money."

"Maybe she does and you don't know it."

I didn't say anything. There was nothing to say.

"You know," Jamila added. "The bank could choose to settle."

"That's always an option."

"I guess it depends on how strong a case they think they have."

"Or how willing they are to throw money at the problem to make it go away," I said. "I'm sure they'd like to keep the security breach quiet."

"Mmmm." I could almost hear the wheels turning in her head. "God, I hate litigation," she said.

"I sympathize. If that boyfriend of hers were still alive, Melanie might have avoided all this."

"Mighty thoughtless of him, to let himself get whacked like that."

"Yeah. The big jerk."

"I'd better run. I've got a conference call."

I made my next call to Aces High, after getting the number from directory assistance. Several rings later, a woman picked up.

"Hi, is Conrad Ash there?"

"Who?"

"Connie Ash. The owner."

"The owner?" she said, sounding surprised. "Nah, he ain't here."

"OK, thanks."

I hit the button to disconnect, using my free hand to pull the little notebook from my purse. I found Connie's name and number from the napkin and tried it. A man answered.

"Is this Connie Ash?"

"Who is this, please?" The voice was pleasant, but terse.

"My name is Sam McRae. I'm an attorney. I understand Tom Garvey used to work for you—"

"A lawyer?" Maybe it was my imagination, but the voice seemed to get tinged with something less than pleasant. "What's this about?"

"I'm representing the person charged with his murder."

No response at first. "He's been murdered?" He sounded astonished.

"That's right."

"And you're representing who?"

"His ex-girlfriend."

"Jesus."

"I understand he once worked for you."

"Yeah. When you said you were a lawyer, I thought maybe he had some beef with me. Man, I can't believe someone killed him."

"Why would he have a beef with you?"

"Oh, man. I just didn't want to do business with him anymore, you know? You just never know. People sue people for the craziest things these days."

"Could we arrange a time to meet?" I hate phone interviews. I like to see the people I'm talking to.

He was so quiet I wondered if he had hung up until he said, "OK."

"If you're available this weekend—"

"I'm available tonight, if you want to come by the house."

"That would be great." I'd never been to Gibson Island, so he gave me directions. He said he would give my name to the man at the guard station, where I would have to check in. Some people live in apartments with doormen. This guy lived on a guarded island.

I went home. A brief scan of the lot outside my apartment building revealed only the usual workaday crowd—hot and tired men and women in wilted suits and uniforms. However, their step had the subtle lift that comes with thoughts of Friday night and the weekend ahead. No black Lincoln.

I fed Oscar, then packed a few items in a paper bag while checking the parking lot like an obsessive-compulsive for the Lincoln. When Oscar was done eating, he jumped on the sofa to crash. I needed to arrange for someone to look after him. I could try to sneak him into the motel, but he probably wouldn't like that, and would protest at the top of his lungs no doubt. Plus I'd have to bring the litter box and food. More stuff to lug around.

I went downstairs to Russell's. He answered my knock wearing a black and yellow paisley satin smoking jacket with a pair of loose-fitting yellow satin pajama pants and holding a scotch and soda. He looked like Hugh Hefner's gay younger brother.

"Russell, can you do me a favor and take Oscar for a couple of days?"

Russell scowled. "Why? Where the hell are you going? You're supposed to be resting, not gallivanting about."

"I have to leave. It's just a couple of days."

"Well, you know how Bitsy will feel about that."

Bitsy was Russell's Scottish terrier, or "Scottish terror," as I called her. In fact, I was surprised she wasn't yapping at Russell's heels. Must have been asleep, thank God. Damn dog could puncture eardrums with that bark of hers.

"Oh, I don't think Oscar will hurt little Bitsy—if she behaves herself," I said.

"Aren't you a stitch?"

"Just keep Oscar in a room. He won't care, as long as you give him food and water. And keep a litter box in there, of course."

Russell wrinkled his nose. "Jesus Christ—a litter box. Why the hell don't you just give me the key and I'll go upstairs and feed him there."

"Because ..." I hesitated. "I'm worried. I don't want to leave him alone. They might hurt him. Those guys who beat me up."

Russell stared. "You think they're coming *here* again? Jesus …
what the hell have you gotten into?"

I didn't know what to say.

He heaved a sigh. "All right. Bring the little bastard down."

"Thanks, Russell. You're the best."

"I know." He tilted his head back with the air of a matinee
idol and stared down his nose at me. "But you'll never get to
find out why." He shut the door.

Chapter SIXTEEN

If you have to be anywhere in Maryland during the summer, it should be on the water. The state's claim to fame is the Chesapeake Bay, the haunt of boating enthusiasts and home to the blue crab, which everyone seems so keen on eating. There's nothing very interesting about the bay. It's a big, flat body of water with a lot of flat land around it. I'd rather have a nice cottage by a scenic river.

I guess Gibson Island has the best of both worlds, in a sense. Strictly speaking, it's not an island, since it's connected to the mainline by an isthmus, but Gibson Almost-Island doesn't have quite the same ring to it. It has the mouth of the Magothy River on one side, the bay on the other. In between, you'll find a lot of fancy houses and people with money.

After checking in with the guard, I followed the isthmus onto the so-called island. From the road, I caught glimpses of houses discreetly tucked behind tall trees, ranging in size and style from country rancher to mini-Buckingham Palace. I turned in at a gated driveway, wove briefly through a grove of oak trees, and emerged in the shadow of a huge house. The road ran in a wide, lazy curve to the entrance, revealing a bluish-green glimpse of water as I took the turn.

The house had an odd, thrown-together look—a stucco exterior with a Spanish tile roof, a kind of Tudor design around the windows, and a front porch, columned southern style and flanked with overgrown hydrangea and roses. If an average person lived there, the place would be ugly. Since the owner had dough, it qualified as unique and eclectic.

I parked beside a gleaming silver Lexus, walked to the front door, and rang the bell. The faint echo of its notes faded out, so the only sound was the hum of a bumblebee. The sweet fragrance of roses saturated the air. I was thinking about ringing the bell again, when the door opened. A fortyish man who looked like a model for Land's End stared back at me. Square-jawed, with neatly combed, brown hair, he wore a golf shirt and a pair of khaki shorts. I guessed he wasn't the butler.

"Sam McRae?" he asked, with a look of pleasant curiosity. "Connie Ash." We shook hands, and he invited me in.

The dark wood lobby looked bigger than my apartment. Dual staircases ran along the walls and a massive crystal chandelier hung from the center of a ceiling two stories high. Ash took me back through a series of rooms furnished in Danish modern, creating as jarring a contrast internally as I'd seen outside. I'm not a big fan of traditional furniture—seems stuffy to me. I could appreciate Ash's desire to decorate for comfort rather than style, although with his money he could've at least redone the house to match the furnishings.

We ended up in a Florida room with a panoramic bay view through floor-to-ceiling windows. A back porch extended off the room for the length of the house. Ash gestured toward a wet bar in the corner.

"Drink? Beer, wine, something stronger?"

"Maybe a soda."

He shrugged. "Name it, I've probably got it. I keep a good stock on hand for parties."

"Ginger ale?"

"Sure." He took out two tumblers, poured me a ginger ale, and a bourbon and water for himself. "Shall we sit outside? It's been muggy the last few days, but tonight it's actually decent."

The porch furnishings were wicker chairs and a red lacquer table. I took a seat. A mild breeze blew off the water, making a set of bamboo chimes clink a haphazard tune. The lawn stretched in a lush green slope to the water's edge, fringed with cattails. From behind one cluster, a pointy-billed blue heron appeared, taking slow, deliberate steps with angular, stilted legs, while scanning the water for dinner.

"This is nice," I said.

"Isn't it? I wouldn't want to live anywhere else." He sank into his chair with a contented sigh. "So ... Tom Garvey's dead and you want to ask me some questions. I'm not sure there's much I can tell you. He worked for me for a while, that's it."

"What kind of work was it?"

"Bringing my computer systems up to date, working on websites, troubleshooting—a little of everything."

"I understand he and Bruce Schaeffer worked together."

"It was Bruce who talked me into hiring him. Begged me, practically. Bruce manages a club for me."

"Aces High, the strip club?"

"Right." If he was embarrassed about my bringing up the nature of the club, he didn't show it. "Anyhow, I guess Tom must have coordinated with him on his work there."

"You don't sound sure."

"I didn't really care how they did it, as long as it got done." He swirled the drink in his glass and took a healthy sip.

"And did it get done?"

"Yeah, far as I know ... at least, at first. In fact, I had him handle some of my other businesses, too."

"But you became dissatisfied with his work?"

"The managers really. They liked him, but sometimes Tom would forget appointments. Or sometimes he was late. Or he'd say you need more RAM or ROM or whatever, but it'd take him two weeks to fix it. Maybe I was too nice. I figured I'd cut the guy some slack—figured he was busy. Plus, he was good at what he did, so I was willing to put up with some eccentricity."

He paused, examining his drink. "Then things really took a turn. Not only was everything taking forever, but I heard he was coming in looking like hell, barely functioning. I thought maybe he'd been working too many hours, staying up too late." He lifted his glass. "Maybe partying a bit too much. Hell, I've been there. Anyhow, one day, I got a call from the manager at one of my dealerships. Tom came in so sloppy drunk, he spent more time harassing the help than doing his work." He shook his head. "Good help is hard to find. I let him go."

"I understand you had an argument with him," I said. "What was that about?"

"It was after I fired him. We had words. He was PO'ed, but I said, look—" He interrupted himself with another swallow, polishing off his drink. "It's business, you know? Care for another?"

I held up the ginger ale, still almost full. "Still working on this one."

"Oh, yeah. Well, I think I'll indulge." He got up with glass in hand and a sway in his gait that made me suspect he might have indulged before I arrived.

When he came back, I asked, "So, how many businesses do you own?"

Ash gazed into space. "Let's see … there's the club, several car dealerships, a couple of restaurants, a storage facility, some shopping centers, a part interest in a mall. I usually have a few real estate deals pending at any given time."

"Other than the club, which businesses was Tom working for?"

"The dealerships and the restaurants. Probably the offices at the mall."

"Probably?"

"Yeah, I think."

I found it interesting that this wealthy guy was so detached from his businesses. Was this what it was like to be filthy rich?

So well-off, you didn't have to think about where the money came from?

"What exactly was the nature of his work?"

He looked at me as if I'd spoken in a foreign language. "I said computers."

"What I mean is, precisely what did he do? Was it just upgrading your hardware? You said something about websites. Was he also setting up databases and which ones?"

"Oh, well." He waved a hand, as if he were shooing flies. "I left it up to the managers to figure out what had to be done. Each business had different needs."

"So you can't say exactly what Tom Garvey was doing?"

"My people kept track of that."

My people? He sounded like a king talking about his serfs.

"You don't seem to take a very active interest in your businesses," I said.

Ash snorted. "Not worth getting worked up over. Let me tell you, I once had a part interest in an investment with an orthodontist and a tax lawyer. The orthodontist was Mr. Mellow. He decided to retire early. Tightened his last retainer, sold us his third, and took off for a condo in Boca Raton. The tax lawyer was the total opposite—couldn't seem to wring enough billable hours out of a day. Then he had a heart attack." Ash snapped his fingers. "Massive coronary. Gone like that. He was only fifty-eight."

"Wow."

"I know. That orthodontist had the right idea—take it easy. Gotta live your life while you can." He dug into his drink, in demonstration of that philosophy.

I watched the heron moving in a slow, stately arc through the shallows. It stopped and cocked its head back, its skinny neck squeezing into an S. With lightning speed, it plunged into the water and came up, a hapless fish caught in its bill. The wind had died, and a faint, musty odor had asserted itself—brine or dead crabs, maybe.

"My client has been charged with identity theft, as well as murder," I said.

"Where you pretend to be someone else, using their social security number or something?"

"Yeah. Identity thieves often get people's personal information from business databases—customer records, employee records. There've been tens of thousands of dollars stolen this way. And Tom was a computer expert."

He blinked. "You think he stole information from my databases?"

"It's possible," I said, trying to ignore the rotting fish smell. "Tom worked for a local bank, the same one that employed my client. They say my client stole the bank's information, but it could have been Tom. And he could have done that to your businesses, too."

He shrugged. "How would I know if he did?"

It was a fair question. The only link the bank had between Melanie and the identity thefts was that box of files, at least as far as I knew. If they'd never found it, would they have made the connection?

"So you're not aware of any sensitive information about your customers or business associates being released?"

"Haven't heard such a thing. Even if someone had that problem, how could they be sure the leak came from my end?"

I had no answer to that one either. With major credit reporting companies having problems with database security, why would anyone look to a car dealership or a storage facility as the source of their credit problems? Personal data is everywhere these days—flying through Internet servers, mined by companies for marketing purposes. Makes you wonder if there is such a thing as privacy anymore.

Sunset tinged the clouds on the horizon pink and orange, in stark contrast to the deepening blue of the sky which the bay mirrored. The heron spread its wings and took off, unhurried and stately.

I finished my ginger ale and said, "Well, I appreciate your time."

"No problem." He gave me a tight smile. "Hope it helped."

He walked me to the door. I gave him a card and we shook hands before I left. I wound my way back to the road, replaying the conversation and thinking. If Garvey was an identity thief, he had a potential gold mine working for an absentee owner like Connie Ash. But Melanie said he had trouble paying his bills. It didn't add up, and that worried me.

I stopped at a Burger King for a quick bite and considered my next move. It was Friday and, as far as I knew, Schaeffer had Friday night off, so I probably wouldn't run into him while making discreet inquiries at Aces High.

One thing held me back—the thought of walking into a strip joint all by my lonesome. It was ridiculous—you would think a woman who has gone into prisons to interview clients could handle a strip club—but I felt intimidated. Other than the help, would I be the only woman in the place? How many drunks would I need to fend off? The things I do for a client.

If I had a companion ... Normally, I'd ask Jamila, but she was representing the other side in one of the cases. She'd probably refuse anyway. Besides, I'd be better off taking a man along. He could pass for a date. Ray was out of the question for a number of reasons. I thought of various male friends, but they were mostly acquaintances and the thought of asking them to come to a strip club seemed worse than going by myself. Russell already thought I was crazy to be involved in this case. Asking him would probably earn me a lecture. Then I remembered Walt Shapiro.

Walt was my mentor at the public defender's office. He had the world-weary, hangdog expression and the cheerfully cynical attitude of a man who's done criminal defense work all his life. He was perfect in almost every way—divorced so he didn't have a spouse to stay home for, adventurous so he'd be inclined to take me up on a spur-of-the-moment invite, and old enough to be my dad. A man who was like a second father to me, who showed me the legal ropes at the start of my career. My intentions would not be misinterpreted.

Now, when I call Walt, it's usually in search of something more conventional in the way of professional counsel. I figured when I told him I needed an escort to a nudie bar, it would catch him off guard a bit. I should have known better.

"Sam, you're a pistol," he said. His characteristic growl sounded positively gleeful. "Anything for a case. Sure I'll go."

"I was thinking about tonight."

"Yeah, yeah, no problem. What the hell? I could use a drink, even a bad one."

I smiled. "I guess the … entertainment doesn't hurt either."

He snorted. "Nothing I ain't seen before. Dump like that, probably pay 'em to put their clothes back on."

We arranged to meet there. Walt said he'd take a cab, because he figured on tying one on.

Aces High was in a fashionable, light industrial section of Route 1, across the highway from a cemetery. Somehow, this struck me as funny, though I couldn't say exactly why. The building was a squat, windowless brick box. The small parking lot was ablaze in yellow sodium lights giving the building a sickly hue.

Walt waited in front. He reminded me of another Walt—Walter Matthau. Or Droopy Dog.

As I got out of my car, I could hear the bass beat of the music, pounding like an amplified pulse from the building.

Walt gave me a wry smile as I approached. "You like adventure, don't you?"

"It would seem so." I surveyed the building. "Not much, is it?"

"Your basic shithole, I'd say." Walt grinned. "Well, anytime you're ready."

I nodded. "Let's do it now, before I change my mind."

Walt pulled the door open, and a cloud of smoke billowed out. The bouncer, an escapee from a punk rock circus who manned a stool near the entrance, gave us a brief, uninterested glance as we walked in. The small, overheated room was packed, and the smell of beer, cigarettes, and B.O. permeated the stale air. The heavy metal tune "Girls, Girls, Girls" blasted from an unseen jukebox.

Although the clientele was mostly male, I was relieved to see women, in groups or with men. Some people sat at tables, but most clustered around a rectangular stage with a pole at either end and a short runway jutting out from the middle. There was a woman at each pole, engaged in something that might have passed for dancing if you had enough drinks. They wore G-strings that were big enough to keep the place from getting shut down and garters for their money. One of them seemed to be enjoying a special relationship with her pole. The other shimmied her torso. Paradoxically, while the torso shook, the breasts didn't. The skin on them was so stretched from her boob job, they reminded me of overfilled balloons. A third woman in a plaid Catholic schoolgirl-cum-slut outfit came on stage and sauntered down the runway to the music.

A small bar was sandwiched between the spectators and one end of the stage. A solo waitress took care of most of the room, although you could also get service from the bartender if you sat at his station.

Walt gestured broadly. "What's your pleasure, seating-wise?"

"How about the bar?"

"You read my mind, sister. Close to the booze."

"Actually, I'm hoping to talk to the bartender."

"Either way, works for me."

Most of the patrons weren't there for the booze or conversation, so it wasn't hard to find a couple of empty stools at the bar. The third stripper had made quick work of losing her schoolgirl outfit and was on her knees, leaning back and thrusting her hips. How athletic. She had better than average fake breasts, but they still stuck out like twin fleshy torpedoes. One guy in the crowd stuck a folded bill out between his fingers, as if hailing a cab, then placed it on the runway. She squirmed her way over to him and picked up the bill, checking the denomination before tucking it into her garter. Then she turned around, suspended her ass about two inches from his face, and launched into a bump-and-grind that would have thrown my back out.

Walt crossed his arms and gazed at the stage, looking amused and bored. "Jesus," he said. "There's enough silicone in this room to make an extra heat shield for the space shuttle."

The bartender looked preoccupied. I hoped he wouldn't mind a bit of chitchat. He was young and skinny, blond with a scraggly mustache. His complexion was so pale, I half expected his eyes to be pink, but they were blue.

"What would you like?" he asked.

"I'll have a ginger ale," I said.

"Christ." Walt barked the word out so loudly, I think even the dancers heard him. "What kind of a drink is that? I'll take Scotch and soda on the rocks." While the bartender got to work, Walt looked down his nose at me. "You're giving the legal profession a bad name, kid. Ginger ale."

"We can't all be world-class drinkers like you, Walt." I noticed, off in a corner, two women giving men lap dances. Actually, the dancing seemed to extend beyond the lap area. I felt like a bit of a perv, but I couldn't help staring with fascination. The women were practically crawling on top of the guys, grinding their crotches as they went. The men sat in plain, wooden chairs, their arms hanging by their sides, dull-eyed and slack-jawed. A beefy man sat to the side, watching. When one man brought his hands up to feel the woman, the watcher came over and said a few words. Down went the hands.

The bartender served our drinks. I leaned toward him and yelled, "Crowded, isn't it?"

He smiled. "An average Friday. You don't come here often, huh?"

"You mean I don't look like a regular?"

"That, plus you don't look like someone scoping the place out for work."

120

"I noticed there were women here, but I hadn't thought about that."

"Some of them are dancers. A few are probably just curious."

He spoke as he worked. His moves were quick and confident, like those of a master chef. He poured the liquor for two drinks simultaneously, a bottle of Seagram's in one hand, bourbon in the other. He pulled the bottles away with a flourish and finished each drink off with mixers.

"You make that look like fun," I said.

He laughed. "You're the only one here who notices."

I glanced at Walt, who gazed at the dancers with detached interest. "You may be right. How long have you worked here?"

"About a year."

"You like it?"

"Not the Ritz, but it pays the bills." He was working on some kind of clear drink now, in a martini glass. A splash of cranberry juice, a wedge of lime, and he handed it to the waitress.

"That's some fancy drink there."

"Now and then, I get a special request. That's when I really have fun. Most of the time, it's just orders for beer or the old booze and soda combos."

He seemed like a nice guy. I figured maybe I could risk asking him a few questions, see what he knew. We had been shouting over the music, so I gestured for him to come closer. He poured someone a beer, then came over.

I leaned toward him. "Is it true that bartenders are also discreet?"

He raised an eyebrow. "Depends."

"I'm an attorney, representing someone in connection with Tom Garvey's murder. If I ask you a few questions, can I count on your ... discretion?"

He looked me over. "Sure." He looked around. "Tell you what, I need to take a break anyway. Can I meet you outside in a few minutes?"

"Fine." I touched Walt's arm. "I'll be outside for a while, talking to the bartender."

Walt drained his glass. "I hope he has a replacement, because I'm going to need a couple more of these."

"I think he's arranging that. I'll be back."

I waited by the front door. I had to say one thing, the lighting in the parking lot was good. I felt quite safe, if a little exposed. I only hoped no one I knew drove by while I stood there.

When the bartender came out, I said, "I feel like I'm on stage, in the spotlights."

He grinned. "Liability concerns. The lighting keeps the crime rate down. Plus it discourages our dancers from engaging in any, shall we say, unauthorized business transactions out here."

I put a hand to my chest, in mock horror. "Prostitution?"

"It can happen. So ... an attorney—a defense attorney, right? Which would mean they've arrested someone for Tom's ..." He looked uncomfortable.

"Yes." I extended a hand. "By the way, I'm Sam McRae."

"Skip Himmelfarb."

We shook hands. He pulled a pack of Lucky Strike cigarettes from his shirt pocket and tapped one out.

"Smoke?" he asked, extending the pack with the red bull's-eye my way.

"No, thanks."

"I quit smoking recently. After I finish this one, I'll probably quit again. It's a bad habit, what can I say? So the police think his girlfriend did it?"

"Why do you say that?" I'd made a point of not saying who I represented.

"Bruce. He keeps saying she did it. Plus, everyone knows about the trouble. You know—how Tom hit her and all."

"What was Tom like?"

"Kind of arrogant, you ask me. One of those ever-so-charming types who get by with a smile and a few well-chosen words." The corner of his mouth turned up in a wry manner. "But he came down a few pegs."

"What do you mean?"

"Something was really eating at him toward the end. Before he was, you know ... found." He paused, taking a drag on his cigarette. "When he started the job, he was cocky, sure of himself. One day he just changed. I don't know, maybe it was his situation at home. He was ... distracted. Short with everyone. Where it really took a toll was his friendship with Bruce."

"Really? I thought Bruce and Tom were close until Tom died."

"They were, but I guess even strong friendships can break down. Bruce hired Tom to work on the computers here. Only gave him the job because he was a friend." Skip jerked his cigarette hand in a derisive gesture. "Like this place needs a computer consultant."

"Why would Bruce hire him if he wasn't needed?"

"To help him out, I think. I heard Tom and he were old friends, and Tom had just come back to Maryland after spending a long time out of state."

"I understand he created the club's website, too."

"Yeah. It's not like he didn't do anything, but I don't think he was all that essential either."

"You'd think the owner would object."

"Owner doesn't really care. Bruce pretty much runs the place. I guess as long as he doesn't run it into the ground, whatever he does is fine."

"So what's Bruce like?"

"All right. I guess he feels like he's got a good thing going here or something. He doesn't seem to have any other ambitions." He shrugged. "Mind you, I'm just speculating. I don't really know him well."

"How do you know their relationship was deteriorating then?"

"Their loud arguments."

"Here? In front of customers?"

"No, no, always in the office. I could hear them through the door when I went back for a case of beer or something. You could hear them over the music, that's how loud they were."

"What did they say?"

"All I heard were voices, not what they said. Then there was this time they were in there going over spreadsheets. They looked kind of worried and were talking low, although no one could have heard them anyway. It caught my eye, so I stood there a moment, watching them."

And no doubt listening, I thought.

"I was going to say something," he said, "when Bruce saw me and got this weird look on his face, like I shouldn't have been there. I figured maybe I should go about my business. So I went into the back room for more beer. On the way out, I noticed the door closed, and they were at it again. Yelling, that is."

"What do think that could have been about?"

"Could have been arguing over his bill, maybe. Seemed funny, though. Don't know why Tom would have been looking at spreadsheets with Bruce."

"Maybe it was something that had to be entered into the computer?"

"Maybe, though I thought he was pretty much done with setting up the computer at that point."

"When was this?"

"Not too long before his, you know." He looked away. "His death."

"It bothers you to talk about it?"

He started to say something, but stopped. Finally, he said, "I've never known anyone who was murdered."

"What were Bruce and Tom working on, if it wasn't the computer?"

Skip shrugged. "Beats me. They were secretive. Always holed up in the office. I couldn't tell you what they were doing."

"When you install a new system, there's bound to be bugs. Maybe they were arguing over how well he did his job?"

"I guess anything's possible, but I don't think so. Far as I know, the computer was working fine. You could ask the assistant manager. She'd know more about that. All I know is, they'd go in that office and wouldn't come out for an hour or more sometimes. Then, one day, Tom stopped showing up."

"Just like that?"

"Yeah. I thought maybe he and Bruce were really on the outs or something, because they always hung together."

Interesting, I thought. Maybe the spreadsheets meant something or maybe not. Maybe Schaeffer's arguments with Garvey were over something that motivated him to commit murder. Or not. I had so little to go on, I couldn't really draw any conclusions. "Was that the last time you saw Tom?"

"He came in once more. It was a few days before he died. He looked like a walking hangover. He hadn't shaved and his hair was greasy. He had dark circles under his eyes, like he hadn't slept for days."

This squared with Melanie's description of Tom when she went to see him for the last time.

"He and Bruce had a little powwow in the office," Skip said. "A very quiet talk. I couldn't hear anything."

"You spend a lot of time by that door, don't you?"

Skip smiled wanly. "It pays to know what's going on around here."

He tossed his cigarette butt away. It bounced off the curb in a brief spray of embers, before it died in the gutter.

"I should get back," he said. "You might want to talk to the assistant manager. She's covering the bar now."

I gave him my card, asking him to call if he could think of anything else, and we walked inside. Walt nursed his drink, staring into space. The assistant manager was bending over to reach something behind the bar. When she popped back up, I recognized her—the woman with Bruce Schaeffer at the gym, the one with the scarred face.

Chapter SEVENTEEN

"Thanks, Rhonda." Skip ducked through an opening in the counter to get behind the bar again.

"No problem." Rhonda didn't see me until I stopped beside Walt. She did a double take, a look of vague recognition crossing her face.

"Kent's Gym," I said.

"Oh, yeah. You're that lawyer, right?"

"Sam McRae. And your name?"

"Rhonda Jacobi."

"Right, I remember now. Got a minute?"

"Sure. Let's go to the office."

"Just a sec. Hey, Walt." I spoke close to his ear, so he'd hear me above the din without my shouting. "You don't have to wait if you don't want to."

He eyed me. "You really don't mind if I go?"

"Nah. I'll be fine."

"OK, if you're sure. Overpriced and underboozed drinks. And Blaze Starr, these dancers are not."

I smiled. "Thanks for coming. Made this a lot easier for me."

"Hey, I had nothing on my busy social schedule tonight."

Walt wandered off, and I followed Rhonda past the rest rooms and down a short hall, gloomy in the light of a single, bare bulb struggling to put out sixty watts. There was a cracked red-and-white exit sign at the end.

The office would have been roomy if boxes hadn't filled most of it. As it was, it could barely hold a wooden desk with an upholstered swivel chair, both of which looked old enough to have been on loan from the Smithsonian, and a folding metal guest chair. Three filing cabinets in mismatched institutional shades of gray and putty lined one wall. Boxes and piles of paperwork filled the rest of the floor space.

Rhonda closed the door, muffling the blaring rock music down to a low throb. She plopped into the swivel chair, which squealed with disapproval. Her somewhat-more-than-zaftig frame wasn't quite right for the black stretch pants she wore. The top three buttons of her white shirt were undone, and while plastic boobs may have been the norm on stage, I got the feeling her décolletage was real. Minus the extra weight and the facial scarring, she could have been out there dancing.

Rhonda gestured for me to take a seat. "Ever find that client of yours?"

"Yes."

"She gonna be OK?"

"I don't know yet."

"Mmm. Good luck with that. What can I help you with?"

"I'm trying to talk to anyone who knew Tom. Maybe get some leads on other suspects the cops might have overlooked."

"I didn't know him, though we did talk from time to time when he came in to work on the system."

"How well do you know Bruce?"

"Not very well. We work different shifts, but we try to touch base every other week or so. More often now, I'd say."

"I guess I assumed you were friends, since you were with him at the gym that night."

She nodded, but said, "No. A problem came up with a delivery. Kind of a pain, because I was on duty that night." An irritable growl edged her voice. "Fortunately, Skip was able to keep an eye on things."

128

"Good that you guys look out for each other. This place isn't exactly crawling with extra help."

She gave a throaty laugh. "No kidding. That's the biz for you. Some places are too cheap even to hire a waitress. Bartender does everything."

The desk had paperwork strewn across it. The computer monitor displayed rows and columns of figures. "Looks like you're having fun," I said.

"Oh, yeah. Between you, me, and the fence post, I'm trying to straighten out another of Bruce's fuckups. Pardon me, but that's what it is. This is one of the reasons I feel like I have to stay in touch with him. This kind of shit's happening more and more often now."

"No offense intended, but how the heck did you end up working here?"

"None taken. And, yeah, managing a strip joint is not exactly what I pictured as my life's work. It's part-time, and it helps pay the bills." She leaned forward. "But I guess you didn't come here to listen to my life story. What can I tell you?"

"Can we keep this confidential?"

"Absolutely."

"I'm interested in finding out more about Bruce's relationship with Tom, particularly before he was murdered."

Rhonda nodded. "Well, Tom got his job here because of his friendship with Bruce. I had the impression they'd known each other a long time. They were having problems though, right before Tom died."

"Can you tell me anything about that?"

"All I know is what Tom told me, and that wasn't much. Sounded like he and Bruce were fighting over money."

"What did he say, exactly?"

Rhonda hesitated, looking slightly uncomfortable. "It's hard to remember. I wasn't taking notes or anything."

"It could be important. Also, the timing. Can you remember what he said and when he said it?"

"I'd have to think. I wouldn't want to pass along bad information." She frowned, staring in front of her as she apparently pondered my question. "OK, here's an example. One time, Tom was here, trying to get one of the programs to work right. He wanted to know something about the financials because they looked screwy, and I told him I'd been having trouble figuring them out, too. And he's like, how do you get your bills paid with a system like this? And I'm like, don't ask me, 'cause I don't have all that much to say about it. Then he makes this sarcastic remark about how he'd better get paid what he's owed. I figure, OK, if Tom hasn't been getting paid regular, maybe he's been cutting Bruce some slack, but now it looks like he's getting pissed off. And, while we're at it, who else isn't getting paid? I'm not here all that much, so sometimes I feel like I'm not really in the loop, you know?"

"Who cuts the checks?"

"Bruce. He won't let me do it."

"Have you had a problem getting paid?"

"No. Probably knows better than to screw around with me."

"Could it just be a personal problem between Bruce and Tom? Maybe Tom loaned him money."

"Well, that occurred to me, but I also know what a mess the books are. So it's hard to say."

Rhonda leaned back again, prompting more caterwauls from the chair. "You know, maybe that's why Tom acted so strange. See, I asked him was there something I could do to help. Well, he got all weird, kind of—I don't know—closed off, all of a sudden. He didn't want to talk about it after that. I didn't pry. I let it drop."

"How long has Bruce worked here?"

"Years, I think. Can't tell you exactly."

"How has he managed, if he's so terrible?"

"That's the funny part. I've been here less than a year, but when I started, everything was fine. It's only been in the last few months that things have gone to hell."

"Would you happen to notice if things fell apart around the time Tom was hired?"

Rhonda looked at me. "You think there's some kind of connection?"

"I don't know what to think. I'm just fishing."

She perched her chin in her hand in a thinker's pose. "You know, now that you mention it, that sounds about right."

"What is it exactly that Bruce is doing wrong?"

"Things just don't add up. I compare statements to stuff on the computer, and nothing matches."

I wouldn't have minded looking at those records myself, although I wasn't sure what they would prove.

"Has the owner said anything?"

"He's hardly ever here. I try to do what I can, but it's not easy, especially since Bruce don't like anyone looking over his shoulder."

"He objects to your reviewing his work?"

"He gets pretty huffy when I ask him about the books, but what am I supposed to do?"

"How often do you work here?"

"Just a couple of nights. Sometimes three." She paused, then gave me a sly look. "I know what you're probably thinking. Why the hell does this part-timer care so much about the bookkeeping in this dump?"

"The thought crossed my mind. I'm assuming the pay is not spectacular."

"You're too right about that. Still, this place has been a good gig for me. It fits my schedule and the extra money don't hurt." She shook her head. "I'd hate to see it go down the tubes, the way Bruce is going."

"What do you mean?"

"Well, Bruce is pretty much in charge here. So far, it's worked out good. The owner shows up once or twice a year, so Bruce feels like he's king of the castle, such as it is. But let me tell ya something." She leaned toward me and I unconsciously followed suit, like we were a couple of high school pals exchanging confidences. "He's really gone off the deep end since Tom died. I'm not sure how much longer he'll be able to handle things. I get the feeling it's going to be up to me after a while. Mind you, I have no interest in taking his place, but I may have to, at least until they get a new manager."

There was a knock at the door.

"Yeah?" Rhonda called. Skip poked his head inside.

"Hey, Rhon, can I grab you a sec?"

"Sure." She took a few moments to close out the computer program she'd been working in, then said, "'Scuse me a moment."

"No problem."

Rhonda left, shutting the door. I looked after her, then at the paperwork on her desk. I wondered how long she was going to be. I waited a few seconds, just in case she came back for something, then got up.

Tiptoeing with exaggerated care to the desk, the theme to the *Pink Panther* running through my mind, I shuffled through the papers. Something caught my attention right off the bat—they were statements for two or three different accounts, issued by First Bank of Laurel.

That didn't necessarily mean anything. Lots of local businesses banked there. One of the accounts had started the reporting cycle with a five-figure sum, then dropped to almost nothing. Another account picked up a large sum, roughly the same amount the first account had lost. I checked the dates. The statements were recent, same month.

Could the accounts be linked to the identity thefts? Or could Schaeffer have been involved in some other shenanigans?

And what did Rhonda really think of all this? She had to think something was rotten at Aces High when she looked at this stuff, particularly since Schaeffer was so secretive. Maybe she was afraid to speak up about it. Or maybe she chose to ignore it. See no evil, hear no evil.

The accounts had Connie Ash's name on them. Did that mean he opened the accounts? Maybe he was more involved with the business than he let on.

I thought I heard a noise outside the door and paused, watching the knob. Feeling pressed for time, I shuffled quickly through other papers on the desk, being careful not to move things.

A phone and a wooden inbox sat to one side. The inbox contained a small stack of papers. The one on top had a yellow sticky note, with *Bruce, What the hell are these? Rhonda* scribbled on it. I took a closer look. It was a printed list of social security numbers with amounts next to them. As I scanned the list, something caught my eye. I thought I saw my social security number.

I heard the rattle of the doorknob.

Chapter EIGHTEEN

I dropped the paper as if it were contaminated and scurried rabbit-like back to the chair. The door opened. Skip was saying something about a delivery.

"That should be here soon," Rhonda said. "They usually come early." She dropped back into her chair and crossed her legs at the knee.

"How about the glassware?" Skip asked.

"Later tonight, probably after we close."

"Great." He looked relieved. "Thanks for taking care of that." He closed the door.

She looked at me and smiled. "Sorry again. Where were we?"

I tore my thoughts from what I thought I'd seen. "Bruce's personal problems since Tom's death. You said he might lose his job?"

"Right, that was it. I think the shock of finding Tom dead in his place did a number on him, 'cause he hasn't been the same since. Always snappin' at people."

"Like at the gym that night with me?"

"Yeah," Rhonda said. "It's been getting worse, too. Last time I saw him, I think he was drunk. We were supposed to have our usual meeting to catch up on things, and he was late. When we did meet, he didn't seem to give a damn about anything. He seems to be less and less involved these days." She sighed. "Someone's gotta run this place."

Both Garvey and Schaeffer seemed to have drinking problems. Was Schaeffer upset because Garvey was dead? Did he kill Garvey? Or was there something else that upset them both?

"I was wondering," I said. "You said the books were screwed up. Would it be possible for me to, you know, take a peek at them?"

She looked guarded. "I don't know ... why would you need to see that?"

"My client has also been accused of identity theft. If it was actually Tom's doing, maybe there's something in those papers," I said, gesturing toward her desk, "something that could help defend her."

"Identity theft?" Rhonda's eyes narrowed. I realized this might be a sensitive subject. She scanned the statements, looking as if she were seeing them for the first time. "Well ... these are business records. I'm not sure Mr. Ash would approve." She opened a desk drawer, seemingly at random, and stowed the papers as if to protect them from my probing gaze.

"It's OK," I said. I had to try, but I couldn't blame Rhonda for trying to protect her boss. "By the way, who was that girl at the gym? The one who yelled at Bruce."

Rhonda's eyes widened, as if the question had knocked her off-balance. "Oh, her? A friend. Knew Tom and Bruce, I guess."

"She also seemed very upset about Tom's death."

"Yeah, she was. I wasn't paying attention, but yeah, she was definitely upset."

"You don't remember anything they said? It seemed like quite a loud conversation."

"I don't know. I think she was just blowing off steam. I think maybe they might have been close at one time. Her and Tom, that is."

"Guess you wouldn't know her name?"

Rhonda shook her head.

I couldn't think of anything else to ask. Maybe about that list of social security numbers, but I didn't want Rhonda to know I'd been through the stuff on her desk. Of course, based on her note, she didn't know anything about it either.

As I got up, my gaze drifted toward the boxes on the other side of the room. "You guys still keeping a paper copy of everything?"

Rhonda glanced over. "Some stuff, yeah, though I couldn't tell you half of what's in there. I think there's a lot of junk that didn't make it into the computer."

"Like what?"

"Hell if I know. This place has been around a while. Some of that stuff could be 50 years old. Me, I'm staying out of it. I've got enough to do."

I nodded. The boxes had the names and logos of various spirits printed on the side. One in particular caught my eye.

"Lobkowicz," I read.

"That's a Czech brewery. Bruce likes unusual beers."

It was the name and a family crest-style logo that had been on the box of files in Melanie's apartment. I felt my pulse quicken.

"Something wrong?"

"Huh?" I shook my head, trying to snap out of it. "No, sorry. I'm trying to think of where I've heard that name before."

"Really? You don't see that ale everywhere."

I shrugged. "Is that right? Well, thanks again."

Out in the hall, someone had propped the emergency exit open, and a warm breeze trickled through the stuffy air. A truck was parked near the door and two guys in T-shirts and jeans were unloading a keg from the back onto a handcart. The storeroom was open. Beyond the truck, a couple of guys leaning against a parked car were having a loud conversation with a third guy, who stood near a line of tall shrubs running along a chain-link fence. He faced away from them with shoulders back, as if at attention. I realized he was taking a whiz into the shrubs and marveled at how the simple act of urination could prompt such good posture.

The lounge area was looking even more like a smokehouse. It was almost eleven and the place was still hopping. Skip was busy, but he looked up and smiled as I approached the bar.

"Can I ask you one more thing," I said. Again, I had to shout over the music.

"What's that?" he yelled back.

"Do you remember ever seeing Tom or Bruce with a woman in her thirties? Wiry with light brown hair? A little shorter than me."

Skip looked blank for a moment. "Come to think of it, I might have."

"You wouldn't know who she is, would you?"

"No, no I don't." Skip looked distracted. He looked back and forth between the drinks he was pouring and me.

"How often did you see her?"

"I can't recall offhand. Maybe once or twice."

"I'll let you get back to work," I said, feeling guilty about interrupting him. "I'd love to talk to that woman, if I can find her, since she's the closest thing to a friend of either of these guys I've found so far."

"I don't remember ever hearing her name. She was just here a couple of times. But if I think of it, I'll let you know."

"Thanks."

I went outside. It was relief to get out of the smoke, to enjoy the relative quiet, other than the buzz of bass notes radiating from the building. Route 1 was empty. Far off, I could hear the stuttered tone of a tractor-trailer braking on I-95.

No one was in the parking lot. Out of idle curiosity, I walked around the building until I found the emergency exit in back. The three men had moved on, but the truck was still there.

That box was helpful, but it still didn't prove anything. Maybe there was a link between the identity thefts and Aces High, but that didn't mean Melanie wasn't involved.

The more I thought about it, the more bothered I became about the list of social security numbers. I wished I'd had time to copy them.

Asking Rhonda probably wasn't an option. I could try sneaking in for another look. Too risky, especially if Rhonda spent a lot of time in the office.

Of course, if I came back at closing time, snuck in, and hid until everyone left, I'd have the whole night, not only to look through the stuff on the desk, but to check out some of the boxes. Maybe there were more files hidden in all that mess.

Sam McRae, attorney at law—specializing in DWIs, bankruptcies, personal injury, and breaking and entering.

Putting the insane thought from my mind, I drove to the motel. The light was off in Melanie's room, and I thought about checking in on her. Through a crack in the curtains, I could see her stretched across the bed, fully clothed, but asleep, looking pale in the bluish-white glow of the TV. I went to my room and tuned in one of the classic movie channels. *The Best Years of Our Lives* was on. I decided to put the in-room coffee maker to good use, although the product would be something less than premium.

Teresa Wright was making breakfast for a confused and hungover Dana Andrews and I was on my second cup of coffee when I called Aces High to find out what time they closed. 2 a.m.

I finished my coffee. This is crazy, I thought. But I had to get back into that office.

I went back and forth on it, considering the pros and cons and ethical problems. In the end, I decided to do it for my own satisfaction, if nothing else. If my social security number was on that list, I had to know.

At 1:30, the movie ended with Teresa and Dana in each other's arms. I checked my luggage. Luckily, I'd chosen a dark shirt for my change of clothes—a T-shirt with a pocket, no less. I stuck my small notebook and a pencil in the shirt pocket, my keys and wallet in my pants. I've often wondered how men manage with just pockets. At that moment, I realized all you had to do was not carry half your worldly possessions with you. By 1:45, I was out the door and on my way to Aces High.

I left my car in the lot of the industrial park next door, taking my flashlight from the glove compartment—just in case. I slid through an opening in the chain-link fence between the two properties.

The building was quiet now. If you concentrated, you could hear the faint sound of interstate traffic, but that was it. Only a few cars were in the parking lot. I crept close to the fence, to avoid the lights, until I reached the shrubbery across from the emergency exit. I stopped behind the tall plants, hoping no one would decide to use them as a bathroom anytime soon.

About fifteen minutes later, a panel truck lumbered into the lot and pulled up to the open back door. The driver got out and went inside. A few minutes later, Skip came out with the bouncer and the driver. The three of them got to work unloading boxes marked *Fragile—Glass.*

I waited, watching them and timing their movements. I didn't know how many trips they'd have to make, but I assumed not many. At one point, when all three were inside, I ran to the door and looked in. The hall was empty. I could hear voices, but they didn't sound close.

Before I could change my mind, I darted down the hall and ducked into the rest room. I got into a stall and sat on the toilet, bringing my legs up so they couldn't be seen if somebody came in. The door closed on its own, but I flipped the lock anyway. I sat there, waiting and hoping for the best.

Chapter NINETEEN

The first thing I noticed was the smell. Made me wish I could have hidden in a supply closet instead. I considered the pros and cons of squeezing into a closet versus the more spacious, but stench-filled, bathroom stall.

I thought about a lot of things as I crouched on the toilet, waiting for everyone to leave. In order for this to work, I was assuming that Ash hadn't bothered to set up an inside alarm system. I hoped his presumed indifference extended to outside door alarms, too. When I was done here, I'd have to get away fast. It could be a silent alarm, so I'd have to move quickly, no matter what. Get to my car. Drive. I'd be the only car on the road, probably. The cops would spot me in a second. I'd need to find a side road, pull over. Then what? Hide in the bushes somewhere for an hour?

That was assuming I'd be able to get out without a key. Do they still have locks that require a key on the inside?

Even if the cops pulled me over, what would they find? I didn't intend to take anything, so there would be nothing in the car to link me to the club. Plus, for good or ill, a white, female in her midthirties didn't exactly fit the police profile of breaking and entering suspects. Still, I couldn't help but feel ridiculous. I was taking quite a chance.

Out in the hall, the sounds of conversation and movement were dying down. A door slammed. I heard footsteps, getting closer. The bathroom door opened. A click and the room went black. The door shut. The footsteps receded.

In the dark, I strained to listen and could have sworn I heard someone talking nearby. I thought it was my imagination, until I heard someone say, "Good night." I waited, I can't say how long. The room was so dark, I felt like I'd disappeared, become a noncorporeal presence in a black hole. I didn't like it, but didn't want to turn on my flashlight until I was sure everyone had left. The hard, but oddly comforting, rim of toilet seat was the only thing keeping me oriented.

Ever since my parents died, complete darkness has made me anxious. I can't sleep without a night-light or some small spark of illumination from a window. I think it was the night in the shelter that did it. I remember when the NYPD came to our apartment in Brooklyn. They explained that my parents were not coming home, because the plane they were on had "gone down." I remember their words. *Gone down.* I wondered if there was a reason they hadn't said it crashed. Maybe "gone down" meant it landed in a strange place, and they just couldn't find it. I asked them about that, several times, until they finally sighed and said "gone down" and "crashed" were the same thing. For a moment, I hated them for giving me that faint hope. Why couldn't they have just told me it crashed?

They took me to a shelter somewhere across the river. I slept in a big room full of cots with other children. It was dark, so dark I might as well have been alone, except I could hear the other kids breathing and the occasional squeak of bedsprings as someone turned over. I kept wondering if it was bedsprings or rats. At times, I thought I felt rats or something, crawling over my bed. When I told people about this later, they said I must have been dreaming. They said the health department would never allow children to sleep en masse in a totally dark room full of rats. Maybe I was dreaming, but that's how I remember it.

Back in the bathroom of Aces High, minutes ticked by. I guess it was minutes, because the darkness had effectively wiped my watch out of existence. I kept listening. Was that someone moving? Was it one last straggler, left behind to lock up? Or was it rats? I shivered. Anything but rats, I thought.

It occurred to me that Rhonda might have locked her office. I put my noncorporeal head in my unseeable hands. I wondered if my brain had disappeared into blank space also. OK, it was possible she didn't feel the need to lock her office. Yes, it would provide an extra level of protection for the computer equipment, but was someone going to break into a strip joint for that? Of course, the office probably had a safe, too. And important files that hadn't made it to the computer.

This was a really stupid idea, I thought.

I heard the rest room door open. Snap. Light washed the room. I blinked and my heart thumped double-time in my chest. The door shut and someone walked my way, coming to a halt outside my stall. Under the door, I saw a pair of worn tennis shoes at the ends of a pair of blue-jeaned legs.

I hadn't even dreamed this dump would merit a security guard. Shit.

Whoever it was tried the door.

I waited.

Then there was a knock. The old bump-bah-da-bump-bump followed by, "Come out, come out wherever you are."

I knew that voice.

"Duvall?" I said.

"Do I have to huff and puff and blow your house in?"

I unlocked the door and yanked it open. The private investigator stood there, grinning.

"This reminds me of that thing they used to say about facing intimidating people. You know, about imagining them in a certain, um, position."

I unfolded my legs and stood up, trying to compose myself, but feeling the heat of a blush in my face.

"What the hell are you doing here?"

Duvall threw back his head and laughed. "Oh, that's good. What the hell am *I* doing here? I could ask you the same thing."

"You don't seem surprised to see me."

"I'm not."

"Well, I'm surprised to see you. Why aren't you surprised to see me?"

"I don't know. Maybe because your car is in the lot next door."

I rolled my eyes. "I guess you would know my car."

"Somehow, I didn't think you had business in the industrial park at this hour. So—"

"So here we are. How'd you get in?"

He held up a set of lock picks. "Not exactly Fort Knox."

"Weren't you afraid of tripping an alarm?"

"There's no alarm. I scoped the place out a while back. I can't find anything that looks like an alarm system, plus they never registered one with the county. Don't worry, I think we're OK."

I sighed. "I hope you're right. I'm putting my license on the line."

"Me, too. It's as illegal for me to be here as it is for you."

"So why are we doing this?"

"I don't know about you," he said. "But I think there's something in that office."

"I know." I stopped, wondering how much more I should say. He noticed my hesitation and smiled.

"Awkward, isn't it?" he said. "We're both ostensibly looking for the truth, but with opposing interests."

"Facts are facts."

"Sure, but some facts would be more convenient for you than others. Like evidence to exonerate your client."

"For all we know," I said, "there may be evidence in there to implicate her further."

"So what do you suppose we'll find behind that door? The lady or the tiger?"

"I don't know," I said. "But we're both here now, and I have a feeling neither of us is leaving until we find out. So let's just do it."

"Spoken like a true pragmatist."

We left the bathroom and walked down the dim hall to the office. The door turned out to be locked, and I silently thanked Duvall for being there. He fiddled at it with the picks, making quick work of it. Once inside, he flipped the light switch.

I went right to the desk. The papers I'd seen were gone, so I checked the drawers, then the in-box. Not there—the bank statements, the piece of paper with the sticky. An almost palpable stab of irritation shot through me. I checked again. Nothing.

"Dammit," I said.

"What's the matter?"

"Ohhh," I groaned. "There was some stuff here earlier. Stuff I wanted to get a closer look at. It's gone now."

Duvall's gaze swept the room like a surveillance camera. "Last time I was here, I think there were more of those boxes," he said, pointing at the ones piled on the other side of the room.

"When was that?"

"About a week ago."

"What were you doing here?"

"Trying to find your client. Apparently, she didn't have a whole lot to do with this place. Not a big surprise, but I thought maybe that woman manager might know who she was."

"You mean Rhonda Jacobi?"

"Yeah. She couldn't tell me much, but while I was here I saw something interesting."

"A box with the word *Lobkowicz* on the side?"

He looked at me. "Right. Same thing that was on the box of files in your client's apartment."

"Are you thinking what I'm thinking?"

"What are you thinking?"

"I think Tom Garvey and Bruce Schaeffer were the identity thieves, not Melanie. I think there may be more files in some of these boxes. How about you?"

"I'll pass on your first thought, go along with your second."

"What's wrong with the first?"

"No proof your client wasn't involved."

"I don't have to prove Melanie wasn't involved, you have to prove she was."

He fixed a level gaze on me. "What makes you so sure she wasn't?"

I filled Duvall in on what I knew. I told him about my trips to Melanie's apartment, and how the box had mysteriously shown up the second time. I told him why she disappeared. And I told him what I'd seen earlier that night. Duvall mulled it over.

"That's interesting," he said. "I can see why you think she was set up. The bank statements don't help though. She worked at the bank."

"So did Garvey."

"True." His hand swept in an arc, toward the boxes. "Shall we take a look?"

"Let's do it."

We dug in. Box-by-box, we worked our way through. It went slowly at first, but the pace picked up as we became familiar with what was in them. Many of the boxes clearly hadn't been touched in years. Opening them sent up a cloud of choking dust. A couple of them were new.

One box held nothing but tax records and a thick file of correspondence with the IRS. A quick glance through the letters showed Ash's returns had been questioned on several occasions.

"Ash seems to have trouble finding good help to handle the books," I told Duvall. I related Rhonda Jacobi's comments about Schaeffer.

"Maybe he doesn't care," Duvall said. "These businesses could provide deductible losses."

"It would explain his lack of involvement. As I understand it, he never comes here."

He shrugged. "In his shoes, I wouldn't either."

We picked up the pace, but the process remained tedious, since we had to view everything together. What if I found something helpful to his case that hurt mine, or vice versa? We also tried to keep track of where the boxes were and put them back as we found them, which took extra time.

We didn't talk much—just stuck to the work, determined to get through it. We had three boxes left when Duvall heaved a great sigh.

"Oh, man," he said. "We're so close, but I've got to stop—stretch my legs." He got up and walked around.

"I know." I stood up, too, and stretched my arms behind me, then overhead. "God, I'm stiff."

From the corner of my eye, I thought I saw Duvall checking me out, but when I looked at him, he'd turned away. I shook my hands out.

"You know, people think investigative work is so glamorous," Duvall said, standing on one foot doing quad stretches, his hand on the desk for balance. "They should see me now. I've spent the entire night in a dingy strip club looking through boxes and come up with nothing."

"Very little, not nothing. We know Ash has tax problems."

"For what that's worth." He switched legs. "Frankly, I'd like to find out more about this Tom Garvey fellow."

"Join the club," I said.

"What about your client?"

"She knows very little about him. He wasn't the kind to talk about himself a lot."

Melanie had said Tom would never talk about his childhood or where he came from. He hardly spoke of work and, when he did, it was always in generalities.

"What about the cops?" I said. "Don't they have information on him?"

"If they do, they're not telling me. According to my source, they have no more information about the mysterious Mr. Garvey than I do."

"What about relatives? Friends?"

"Garvey seems to have been short of both. Apparently, he had no next of kin. Strange since he was pretty young."

"I don't have any next of kin," I said.

"No parents? No siblings?"

"My parents died when I was a kid. An only child."

"Who raised you?"

"A cousin. Couldn't tell you where she lives now." I knew Addie was out West somewhere, but her exact address seemed to change with the phases of the moon.

He shot a curious glance my way. "Huh. Well, I need to start digging into Garvey's past a bit. I'm a little curious about the Mob connection in this case, too, though I haven't given it much attention. Doesn't seem to pertain to the identity thefts."

"What do you know about it?"

"All I know is that FBI agent is bound and determined to find some guy named Gregory Knudsen." Duvall snorted. "He seems to think Knudsen has the answers to all his questions, whatever they are."

"When I was at Melanie's the first time, I found a key for a P.O. Box in my name," I said. "And inside that box, there was a letter addressed to Gregory Knudsen. Could he have something to do with the identity thefts?"

He shrugged. "For all we know, he could have killed Garvey."

"Garvey had some connection with Knudsen. I think Jergins said they were friends or something. I don't suppose Jergins has dropped any subtle clues your way about what Knudsen might have to do with all this."

Duvall hooted with laughter. "Agent Jergins is about as subtle as a rhino in heat. And he doesn't exactly share his innermost thoughts with me. He's driving the detective nuts."

I smiled, feeling sorry for Derry who was the type to hold his frustrations inside. If he had a pet, I hoped he wasn't kicking it every time he came home from work.

"Last I heard, Jergins was trying to follow up on a lead in Baltimore," Duvall continued. "Some guy named Ryan Bledsoe who went to school with Knudsen. I heard he didn't get anywhere with him. All Jergins had to say was FBI, and Bledsoe told him to take a hike."

"That's interesting," I said. "I wonder if he does know something."

"You could always ask him," Duvall said. "He lives in Rosedale, I think."

Duvall spelled out Bledsoe's name, as I wrote it in my notebook. We both turned, reluctantly, back to the remaining boxes.

"Let's finish it," I said.

Chapter TWENTY

By about four thirty, we were done. Outside, the air felt warm and liquid, the heat of the previous day lingering. For exercise, we bypassed the shortcut and walked the dirt shoulder of Route 1 to the lot next door.

The only sound in the predawn stillness was a robin, sending out its two-note singsong from a stand of trees in the cemetery across the street. Under a streetlight, an opossum, about the size of my cat, nibbled on the grass. As we drew closer, the possum froze on its back legs, in alert mode, then scampered off into some brush. Apparently, possums don't always play possum.

When we reached the cars, we paused before getting in. "Well," Duvall said. "It's been real."

"Yeah, sure has."

He peered at me. "You OK? You look beat."

"I'm fine." I gave him my plucky can-do smile, but I was a little punchy from looking through all those boxes. My stomach gurgled.

"OK." Duvall hesitated. "Well, I'll see you around."

"Take it easy." I watched him unlock his car. "Hey, Duvall."

He looked up.

"I never did thank you for your help. I couldn't have gotten in the office without you."

"You're welcome," he said.

We lingered a moment longer, then got in our cars and left.

Normally hectic, Route 1 was quiet and empty now. I resisted the giddy urge to blast down the road, figuring a cop on the graveyard shift was probably lurking somewhere. The darkness seemed like a perfect complement to the dreary landscape, largely comprised of junkyards, industrial buildings, and strip shopping centers, with generic signs advertising beer/wine, deli, and dry cleaning. Now and then, a mom-and-pop budget motel from pre-interstate days could be seen, crouching in dark disuse amid the architectural clutter—crumbling anachronisms that seemed to exist only because no one had the energy to tear them down.

Traffic picked up as I neared the I-95 interchange, particularly panel trucks and tractor-trailers making early morning deliveries, or heading for the Jessup truck stop. Then the lights of a twenty-four-hour diner beckoned and my stomach growled again. In the battle between fatigue and hunger, hunger won.

Frank's Diner was a traditional glass-and-steel affair, the kind of place where every booth has a jukebox, and the waitresses wear plain, starched uniform dresses and call you "hon" in the Baltimore tradition. The fluorescent lights created a surreal glare on the Formica tables and windows. The only sounds were the occasional clink of utensils on plates and the waitress talking to customers. I slid into a booth, checked the menu, and quickly settled on a waffle, bacon, two eggs over easy, an extra side of toast for dipping, and coffee.

The place had four other customers. A jowly man with gray hair and slits for eyes, wearing a T-shirt and a red billed cap with a Chevy logo, sat in a corner booth and sucked down coffee like an emphysema patient taking hits of oxygen. No doubt driving the tractor-trailer parked outside. Two cops—one male, one female—shared a quiet conversation at the counter. I'd have expected them, but not the twenty-something guy dressed in "office casual," tapping on his Palm Pilot. Maybe he was a salesman. Maybe he worked odd hours in an office. You never knew who would be in a diner during the wee hours of a Saturday morning or why. I doubt anybody would have guessed I'd just spent the night in a strip club.

I sipped coffee and thought about what I'd learned. I knew Schaeffer and Garvey had to be part of the identity theft scheme. If only I'd found something concrete. I could have kicked myself for not stealing that list of social security numbers while I had the chance. Why was I so damned honest?

My food arrived, and I dug in with gusto, polishing it off in record time. What about Knudsen? Why was Jergins so interested in him? Why wouldn't Ryan Bledsoe, that guy in Baltimore, answer any questions? Maybe I'd have more luck. Some people don't like talking to cops, plus Jergins had the social skills of a tree stump. Anyway, Bledsoe was the only lead I had left, other than the woman with no name at the gym.

Dawn had broken by the time I got back to the motel. I undressed and fell into bed, not even brushing my teeth.

For a long time, I lay there, staring at the inside of my eyelids. The coffee hadn't been a good idea. I was wide awake-exhausted, the same thoughts dancing at the edge of my consciousness with the unwelcome sensation of a recurring bad dream. I'd open my eyes to see by the glowing red numerals of the motel clock radio that another ten minutes had crept by, then close them again. Just when I was starting to think it would never happen, sleep came.

φ φ φ

The phone rang. I ignored it until it stopped. I kept my eyes closed, willing myself to relax and drift back to sleep.

The phone rang again. I opened my eyes. It was almost two. I remembered where I was and why I was there. I rolled over and snatched up the receiver. "What?"

"Sam?" It was Melanie. "I'm sorry. Did I wake you?"

I grunted in reply.

"Did you get my note?" she asked.

"Note?"

"I guess not, huh? I checked out this morning. I'm staying with my friend, Karen. Her address and phone are in the note."

I cleared my throat. My mouth tasted like tobacco-flavored scum.

"Sam?"

"Yeah."

"You OK?"

"Sure." My voice was hoarse from secondhand smoke. "I was out late. Just tired."

"Did you go to the club?"

"Yeah." I saw no harm in sharing what I'd learned, though I figured I'd skip the little details about trespassing. "Found some interesting stuff. Aces High has accounts at First Bank of Laurel. It looks like money is going back and forth between the accounts for reasons that aren't obvious to me."

"I'm not sure what that means."

"I'm not sure what it means either. It's not money laundering, because that involves hiding money under other names. Aces High and Connie Ash were named on all the accounts."

"So why move the money around at all?"

"Got me. I also saw a list of social security numbers and thought I saw mine on it."

"Bizarre. Are you sure it was your number?"

"I can't be positive. I was kind of going through stuff on the desk while Rhonda was out, and she came back in the office before I could get a good look."

"Rhonda?"

"You know her?"

"Tom mentioned that name. I don't think he liked her."

I could picture Rhonda being the type who could rub a person the wrong way.

"I think I'll head up to Baltimore today," I said. "I've got a lead on Gregory Knudsen. Did Tom ever mention knowing anyone in Rosedale or anywhere in Baltimore?"

"No."

After we hung up, I stretched and yawned. Outside, a maid's cart rumbled by. Doors were opening and closing. The sun glared through a gap in the utilitarian floral drapes. For the first time, I got a good look at the room. Not fancy, but who cared? Hell, add a fridge and I could live here forever. The carpet might have a few stains, but the place got cleaned regularly—more often than I cleaned my apartment.

I got up to use the bathroom and saw Melanie's note. I felt a bit nervous for her. I hadn't wanted to leave her locked up, but maybe she would have been safer in jail. Maybe—secretly—I *was* a little concerned about her trying to flee again. I wasn't her keeper. If she wanted to run, she'd find a way. Stavos had me worried though. If he were willing to torture me to find Melanie, what would he do if he found her?

I brushed the scum off my teeth and showered, then got dressed. My next move was to find Ryan Bledsoe, who was in Rosedale, wherever that was. Somewhere in the Baltimore suburbs. That's all I knew. I had a Baltimore map at home. Better still, I could get directions off the Internet. But I wasn't sure about going there. If I called Russell to ask whether he saw the Lincoln in the parking lot, he'd probably pepper me with questions and unwanted advice. He was a sweet man, but worse than a mother hen. I could go to the office, but Stavos had to know where that was, too. The office would be empty. The apartment building wouldn't.

I decided to risk a quick visit to my apartment.

Half an hour later, I parked outside my building, scanning the lot once more. I didn't waste any time getting out, locking the car, and making a beeline for the door. I was so intent on getting inside, I didn't hear him behind me.

"Hey," he said.

I must have jumped like a pro basketball player doing a layup. I swiveled round and saw Ray.

"Christ Almighty." My heart was trying to pound its way out of my chest.

"I'm sorry. Didn't mean to startle you."

"*Startle* is hardly the word. Where's your car?" Guess I'd been too busy looking for a certain other car to see it.

"I'm parked farther down. Can we talk?"

I nodded. Ray followed me upstairs. The morning paper lay before my door, looking unmolested. I kicked it inside and tossed my purse on a chair.

"Coffee?"

"Sure," he said.

I trudged into the kitchen and went through the motions. Normally, Oscar would be circling my feet, trolling for food. I missed the little asshole.

Ray perched on one of the breakfast barstools, looking at me with astonishment. "At the risk of offending you, you look like hell."

"Mmm. Long night. So … you came quite a ways to talk. You want something to eat?"

"I can't stay long. I told Helen I was bowling."

"Bowling? How very … down to earth. An interesting excuse."

"Not completely out in left field. I'm in a league."

"Ah." Another little factoid I'd never known about Ray. Things we never talked about, because we were so busy fucking.

Ray paused to examine a salt shaker. "I've been thinking about it, and maybe you're right. Maybe the case should be reassigned to someone else."

I looked at him. "But this case means a lot to you."

"You mean something, too."

Oh, please, I thought. I turned away, pretending to search for something in the cupboard. "I don't know, Ray."

He didn't say anything. I pulled out a jar of peanut butter and began making toast. I poured two cups of coffee. He took the one I offered him, looking solemn. I got out the milk and sugar.

Ray poured milk into his coffee. "Were you with someone last night?" he asked, sounding tentative. "Is that why you were up late?"

I shook my head. "No, that's not it. Look, we were always friends. My biggest fear was this would ruin our friendship."

His eyebrows drew together, as if he were trying to solve a complex math problem in his head. "It's not just about sex, you know."

"Really? What else is there?"

"We have a good time. At least, I thought we did."

I smiled, though I felt no great pleasure. "Yes, but … something's missing. I don't feel like I know you."

"What's there to know?"

"Do we ever really talk about anything other than work?"

He considered this. "I thought we did. What's wrong with work?"

"Nothing. It's just … I don't know. I can't put my finger on it. It's like there's this gap between us and I can't cross it."

Ray nodded. He looked at me. "You're not exactly easy to get to know either."

I thought about that. "I guess you're right. I suppose we have that in common. Still, I didn't know you bowled. What's your average, anyway?"

"One forty-five."

"That stinks."

He smiled. "Not in duckpins. It's very high in duckpins."

"See, I didn't know that."

We sipped our coffee.

"Maybe this is silly," I said. "But it bothers me that I don't know what we are. Friends? Lovers?"

"Both?"

"Can we be both?"

His eyes met mine, then looked away. Neither of us wanted to follow up on that thought. I ate my toast, sorry I'd mentioned anything, but glad it had finally come out.

Ray glanced at his watch. "I guess I should go." As he slid off the stool, he said, "Thanks for the coffee. I don't know what I'm going to do about the case yet."

I ran my finger along the counter, picking up nonexistent dust. "Well, use your best judgment. Hell, it's really not *that* great a case, is it?"

"Murder and identity theft, with the local police and two federal agencies tripping over each other? Yeah, it's a real delight."

I managed a genuine smile this time. "Maybe you can enlighten me on something."

"I'll try."

"Two things, actually. What's the connection between the Mob guy from New York and the case? I take it the murder wasn't a Mafia hit. Is the Mob involved in the identity thefts?"

Ray looked bemused. "Not as far as I know. The Mob guy is Jergins' obsession, but no one else seems to care."

"Yet that guy he's looking for—Knudsen—he has some connection to this, right?"

"I guess so. Again, Jergins is the one you'd have to ask."

"Yeah, I'm sure he'd tell me," I said. "The other thing is Bruce Schaeffer. He was out of town the weekend Garvey was killed, right?"

"Right. His family says he was visiting."

"So they might lie for him."

"Other people corroborate his story, not just his family."

"And Melanie was the only one who saw Garvey that weekend?"

"Well—" He looked at me.

"Well, what?"

"This is something I'll have to give you anyway, so I'll tell you. Hers were not the only fingerprints at the scene."

"Really?" Nice of the cops to leave that bit of information out. Cops have that nasty habit sometimes.

"There was another set of prints, unidentified."

Fascinating. A mysterious visitor meeting the mysterious Mr. Garvey. Who could that be?

Chapter TWENTY-ONE

After Ray left, I washed the dishes and looked up Ryan Bledsoe online. When I called, a woman I figured was his wife answered, sounding breathy and distracted. I explained who I was and what I wanted, and she told me Ryan wasn't there.

"Could I leave a message?" I asked. On the other end, I could hear a child babbling in the background and a baby squeal. I couldn't tell if it was in joy or pain.

"Well, sure, but you might want to call him at the dealership. See, we were supposed to go to the ocean today," she said, giving the *o* in ocean the typical, Baltimorean emphasis, "'cept the dealership called him in unexpected. I'm trying to pack and all, so we can hit the road when he gets home. Kirsten? Kirsten, put that down."

"How late will he be there?"

"They close at six, but you should call him right now, I think."

"I'm heading up there anyway," I said. "Maybe I could swing by the place and talk to him."

"If you think that's best," she said, sounding a little uncertain. "Will this take long?"

"No, I just prefer to talk to people in person."

"It's that we're *supposed* to be in Ocean City right now. If it weren't for work, we would be. I know he's trying to leave as soon as possible."

The baby let out another whoop. She pulled the phone from her mouth, but not far enough to keep me from hearing her clearly. "Kirsten, stop that. Don't wave that thing at little Dodo." She came back, picking up where she'd left off as if nothing had happened. "He might even leave early, I don't know."

I couldn't stop myself. "Dodo?"

"His name is Tommy, but Kirsten calls him Dodo." She started rattling on about kids and their pronunciation and so forth. I checked the clock.

She paused for breath, and in the interest of cutting the child development lesson short, I asked, "Where's the dealership?" so fast, it sounded like one word.

She gave me the name and an intersection. Even as we spoke, I was looking it up online. "Thanks for your help."

"Sure. He's supposed to be there 'til six. Maybe call first, to make sure he hasn't left."

"OK, thanks. Bye."

"Bye." As she hung up, I heard her cry out, "Stop that, stop that *now*." Sounded like it was going to be a fun trip to the beach.

Simpson Motors was on Pulaski Highway. Like Route 1, Pulaski was a showcase of Rust Belt economy—more junk yards, more tire and transmission shops, more fast food, and more decaying motels, interspersed with modern box stores like Home Depot and Circuit City. The dealership was at a busy corner, marked by a string of pennants in carnival colors, looking limp and dissolute in the afternoon heat. Rows of new cars glared with the monotonous pattern of the sun's reflection.

Inside the glassy, air-conditioned showroom, a few customers drifted around, idly checking the display models, while men in suits watched them the way lions might watch zebras. I headed toward a small knot of suits hanging around the offices drinking coffee and acting like they'd just met at a dull party. The way a couple of them looked at me, you would have thought I was the hired stripper.

"Hi, I'm looking for Ryan Bledsoe," I said.

Heads turned toward a guy in a dark gray suit and a skinny black tie, with brown hair moussed into a modern do that said, *"This is not your father's auto salesman."* Bledsoe must have been in his thirties, but he looked about ten years younger. He blinked at me from behind glasses with thin, rectangular frames, giving him a mild-mannered, slightly geeky persona.

"Could we talk somewhere private?" I asked, handing him my card upside down.

He read it, ignoring the other boys' stares. Looking puzzled, he said, "Mind if we go outside?"

"Fine."

As I followed him, I could hear low voices and laughter behind us. Bledsoe seemed to care what they thought as much as I did. In the back parking lot, we sat in the building's shadow on an old picnic bench someone had thoughtfully placed along the wall and watched cars navigate the McDonald's drive-through next door.

"So," I said. "Those offices you use for customer negotiations—they really are bugged then?"

Bledsoe managed a weak smile. "Am I being sued or what?"

"Actually, I'm representing a woman who's been accused of murdering Tom Garvey. Did you know him?"

He shook his head. "Should I?"

"He had a friend named Gregory Knudsen. You know him, right?"

Bledsoe stared at me, his expression transforming from geeky to threatening. "Any friend of Knudsen's is no friend of mine," he said, the hint of a snarl in his voice.

"You went to school with Knudsen. Was it college? High school?"

He squinted at me. "Are you with the cops?"

"I'm an attorney, like the card says."

"So why all these questions?"

"I told you. I'm representing someone accused of murder—"

Bledsoe shot off the bench as if it were red-hot. "Well, I don't know anything about it." His voice had raised a notch, in volume and tone. "I haven't seen Greg Knudsen in years and I'd like to keep it that way."

"You were friends once. In school?"

"Yeah, high school. So what? I knew plenty of people in high school. That doesn't mean I know them now." Bledsoe started to walk off.

I followed. "This could be important," I said. "I'm representing an innocent woman."

"Sure you are."

"I swear. Look, you're my only lead, OK? You wouldn't want to protect a killer, would you?"

His hand was on the door, but he stopped and turned toward me. "There was a cop asking me about Knudsen, but he never said anything about murder. Besides, if there's one thing I've learned, it's never to get involved."

I waited a few beats, giving him the kind of look I'd give a jury if I ever defended a death penalty case. "I don't know about that cop. All I know is, my client's life is at stake. Your name wouldn't even have to come into it. I just need to get some background information on this guy. If Knudsen's a murderer, don't you want justice done?"

Bledsoe mulled it over. Of course, I had no reason to think Knudsen was a murderer. I was just pulling out all the stops. It worked, because he finally walked back to the bench and sat down, leaning against the wall and staring before him in a defeated way.

"Shit," he said. "Gregory Knudsen. After all these years, I can't believe I'm hearing that name again. Twice in two weeks, no less."

I sat on the other end of the bench. "Why do you hate him?"

Bledsoe said nothing for a moment. "Look, I don't know how any of this can help you. This is all ancient history, you know? I haven't seen Greg Knudsen in ages, but back then, he was nothing but trouble—he and Bruce Schaeffer."

"Bruce Schaeffer," I said. "So Bruce was also friends with Knudsen?"

"Yeah, we all hung out together. Don't tell me he's involved, too?"

"I don't know, but maybe."

He leaned forward, propping his elbows on his legs, and rubbed his face, looking tired. "I can't say I'm surprised they're involved with a crime, but murder?"

"And you don't recall them hanging out with anyone named Tom Garvey?"

"I don't remember anyone at school by that name."

"So tell me about Schaeffer and Knudsen. You said they were trouble?"

"They liked to pull stunts. They were pranksters, really. I met them in junior high. We did the usual—threw firecrackers into the girl's room, smoke bombs in the teachers' lounge. Stupid stuff. But I stopped hanging with them in high school, when things started getting a little too serious."

"What do you mean?"

"Their tricks just got too wild for me. By the time we were juniors, they'd graduated to cherry bombs and M-80s. They were the twin terrors of Dundalk High. Seemed too risky to be friends with them. I planned to go to college." He shook his head. "Glad I dropped them, too, after what happened."

"What was that?"

"They set up something to explode in the chemistry lab. Set it on fire. There was a rumor around school that it killed a kid, but I think that was bullshit." He closed his eyes and put his hand over them, as if shutting them weren't enough. "Still, they *could* have killed someone. Made me sick. Like, how could I have been friends with these guys?"

He opened his eyes again. "They'd been suspended a few times, and that was the last straw. Both of them were expelled."

"Was that the last time you saw them?"

Bledsoe's jaw clenched. "I saw them around after that. I lived with my parents in Dundalk while attending community college. They had nowhere to go, so I'd see them at parties sometimes. I think people invited them because their past was so checkered. It fascinated them. Like a couple of circus freaks." He snickered without humor. "Losers."

"Do you know anything about what they've done since then? I'd really like to talk to Knudsen, if you know where he is."

"I haven't seen them since college, and I don't ever want to see them again."

"You seem pretty bitter."

"I have my reasons."

"Which are?"

Looking resigned, he said, "I had a girlfriend. We'd been going together a year or so. A real sweet kid. A little naive, maybe. Somehow or other, she ended up getting involved with Greg and dumping me. I always thought Greg seduced her to get back at me for snubbing him and Bruce. Greg could have his way with practically any girl. He was amazing that way. He could probably talk a nun out of her habit."

He paused. "I lost touch with her after that, but I heard years later that Greg knocked her up, then left town—split the friggin' state, in fact. She was a strict Catholic, so abortion—" He shook his head. "Out of the question. But he left her high and dry. That's the kind of wonderful guy he was."

Neither of us spoke. Someone yelled an order for a Big Mac and a Coke, and the drive-through speaker rasped in response.

"I heard she wasn't the same after that," he added. "I heard she flipped out, became obsessed with getting Greg back for a while. When he didn't come back, it really changed her. Made her bitter."

"What was her name?"

"Barbara Ferrengetti."

"Do you know if she still lives in the area?"

"I never tried to look her up. To be honest, I don't really want to know."

Chapter TWENTY-TWO

One of the dealership phone directories listed B. Ferrengetti in Dundalk, the only Ferrengetti in the book. Dundalk was an aging suburb, southeast of Baltimore, close to Sparrows Point and the Bethlehem Steel Mills.

I retraced my route on the Baltimore Beltway to the last exit before the Harbor Tunnel, which dumped me into a neighborhood where the overall theme was old, cramped, and brick. I stopped for directions at a firehouse, wedged between a funeral home and a liquor store. Despite the urban setting, the smell of water from the Outer Harbor and the seagulls that cried overhead gave the place an odd touch of the beach.

Barbara lived on a street of identical, rectangular, brick houses, paired off and mated by common walls, each a mirror image of the other. Several of the porches had painted metal awnings and were decorated with hanging geraniums and petunias—probably to make it easier for the residents to figure out where the hell they lived. Whatever restrictive covenant required the fronts to look the same apparently didn't apply to the backs. The alleys were a visual cacophony of telephone poles, clothes lines, and fences of various heights and materials.

I parked in the first space I found and walked to Barbara's house. In front, a short, wiry woman with an array of plastic grocery bags around her feet bent into the back of a new SUV. She grunted with effort as she reached for something, but all I could see was a skinny ass in cutoffs and pale white legs. She wore red plastic flip-flops.

I cleared my throat. "Barbara Ferrengetti?"

"Hold on." With the Baltimore accent, it came out sounding like *hold awn*. A few seconds later, she popped up with an errant can of vegetables in hand. Closing the SUV, she turned toward me.

It was the woman I'd seen outside Schaeffer's apartment, the one arguing with him at the gym. Blue eyes that showed no recognition blinked at me above a pointed nose. Worry lines creased her brow. Despite a thin face, her cheeks seemed to droop, pulling her mouth into a permanent frown.

"Yeah?" she said, her tone conveying the clear desire to dispense with me and get on to the next tiresome chore.

"Hi," I said. "My name's Sam McRae. I'm an attorney—"

"Are you from the workers' comp? Cause you're supposed to talk to my lawyer."

"I just want to ask some questions—"

"Nuh-nuh-nuh-nuh-no." She waved a hand to cut me off. "My lawyer said you gotta talk to him." Suddenly conscious of the fact she was waving a can of food around, she put it in one of the bags and began rubbing her wrist.

"Are those heavy?" I said. "I could help you get them inside."

She looked me over, perhaps wondering if this were a test of her alleged disability. "That would be nice. I mean, usually I have to make several trips 'cause of my wrist, or my son helps. But since you're here."

We gathered the bags—she made a great show of wincing on picking hers up—and I followed her up the steps and into the house. The kitchen was straight back with the living room off to the left. I stopped briefly to gawk at her wide screen, high-definition TV—fifty inches, at least. She also had a state-of-the-art home theater sound system, made up of several little speakers scattered about the room. A workers' comp award for carpal tunnel wasn't going to cover that lot. In contrast, her sofa and chairs looked like they came from the Salvation Army. A carved wood crucifix hung on the wall.

She took her bags to the fridge, where she unloaded a half gallon of milk and several packages of deli meat. I checked mine for perishables and found iceberg lettuce and frozen orange juice which I handed to her. The kitchen was small—the decor, circa 1950. Over a small table, I spotted a picture of Jesus, with a passage of scripture in fancy print underneath. Blessed art the clever, I thought, for they shall rip government agencies off to provide for their needs.

"Just leave the rest," she said. "My son will help later."

"Barbara, the thing is, I'm not from workers' comp."

She froze and stared at me. "What?"

"My name is Sam McRae and I'm an attorney, but I'm not here about your workers' comp claim."

"Well, what the hell *do* you want?"

"I need to ask you about Gregory Knudsen."

Barbara's eyes narrowed. "Who do you work for?"

"I'm defending the person accused of killing Tom Garvey."

She didn't say anything. She stood there, breathing at me, looking ready to bolt from the room any second.

"You knew Tom Garvey, right?"

Nothing.

"And you knew Gregory Knudsen in high school?"

More nothing.

"I understand you had his child."

Barbara peered at me. "Where do you get all this?"

"Does it matter? I'm trying to find Knudsen. Do you know where he is?"

She crossed her arms. "No."

"I was told he left the state?"

"Yeah."

"Do you know where he went?"

"No."

"Have you heard from him since?"

She paused a few beats. "No."

"Do you know if he's still friends with Bruce Schaeffer?"

A longer pause. Her upper lip began to twitch. "I have no goddamned idea."

"Have you stayed in touch with Bruce since high school?"

She didn't answer.

"Did they know Tom Garvey then?" I said.

A ripple of some emotion ran through her expression, but I couldn't finger it. Confusion? Doubt? "No."

"You're sure they didn't know Tom Garvey?"

"I don't know. I don't think so."

"When did they meet him?"

"How should I know?"

"How do you know they didn't know him then?"

She shifted from one foot to the other. I was getting to her. Or maybe she just had to go to the bathroom. "I don't know."

"How did you meet Tom? Did Bruce introduce you?"

Barbara pursed her lips. "I think I've answered enough questions."

The front door opened and closed. A few seconds later, a tall young man came in. He was attractive with a healthy head of light brown, curly hair and blue eyes that girls used to describe as dreamy. His mild, curious gaze glanced off me, but he didn't look at Barbara. She kept her eyes averted from him as well, her expression flat. The young man walked to the fridge, opened it, and retrieved a Tupperware drink container. Then he put the spout to mouth, tipped his head back, and took a long swig.

"Dinner's at six," she said.

He finished his drink, then wiped his mouth with the back of his hand. "Going out."

"Suit yourself."

He shut the refrigerator, a trifle too firmly, and strode out. As we listened to him trot upstairs, she took a deep breath, then released a long, tired exhalation.

I took out one of my cards. "If it's OK, I'll leave this with you."

Her eyes were closed now, as if to shut out reality. I put the card on the counter and let myself out.

ϕ ϕ ϕ

Even if Barbara was scamming workers' comp for extra bucks, I didn't picture her making the kind of money she'd need to afford an SUV or high-dollar home entertainment system. Maybe she was in on the identity theft scheme. Did her argument with Bruce have something to do with that? And what about Knudsen? The subject of Tom Garvey seemed to get under her skin. At the gym, she'd acted upset to hear Tom was dead. *You're trying to protect him.* That's what she'd said to Schaeffer. Protect him from what?

Before going home, I decided to run by Schaeffer's and take another crack at questioning him, or at the very least, see how he reacted to the questions I asked.

I climbed the steps to Schaeffer's apartment again and knocked on the door. No one answered. I tried again. While I was waiting, the door to my left opened. The red-faced, balding neighbor peered out. This time, he wore Bermuda shorts with his ribbed tank top. Black socks and a pair of women's nylon slippers. Very tasteful.

"Hello again," he said. The garlic was, thankfully, absent from his breath this time, but I could smell the beer.

"Hi."

"Struck out, huh?"

"Guess so. You wouldn't know where he is this time, would you?"

"Saturday night? Probably working. He'll be off tomorrow though."

I smiled. "You seem to know his schedule pretty well."

"That I do. Like to keep tabs on what goes on. Pays to keep your eyes and ears open."

"Mmm-hmm. I guess the cops have been pretty grateful for your help. On the murder, that is."

"Cops?" He looked disgusted. "Who said anything about cops?"

"You didn't tell the cops you saw a woman here the weekend the murder took place?"

"Hell, no. I never talk to cops. See, it also pays to never get involved." He laughed, in a dry, breathy rasp. "I didn't say nothing about his lady callers that weekend."

"Lady callers?"

"You know." He winked in a way that made me want to take a hot shower. "Roommate's out of town. He has a few ladies over. Different times. Everyone's happy."

"Sure. Did one of the ladies have brown hair? Come by in the middle of the day on Saturday?"

He looked wary. "You're not a cop, are you?"

"Lawyer." I found one of my cards and gave it to him. "I represent the lady with brown hair. Cops think she killed the guy."

"No." He looked shocked. "I remember her plain as day. I heard them talking when she left. They was jawing for a while. She was kinda upset about something."

"You're sure it was him?"

"Positive. Saw him through the peephole."

"You said he had another visitor? A lady?"

"Two, I think. They came by real late."

"Two ladies?"

"Well, sure." He issued another high, thin laugh. "You know. Double your fun." He gave me that wink again. I wanted to rub myself down with Clorox.

"What did they look like?"

He licked his lips. "Well, now, I didn't actually see them. I heard one of them laughing. Just happened I was up. I get up three times a night to take a whiz."

More information than I needed. "When was this?"

"It was that Saturday night. Sunday morning, really."

"And you never saw who it was?"

He shook his head. "Nah. By the time I got to the peephole, they'd gone."

"So you couldn't say for sure that it was two women?"

"Well, I didn't see 'em, but that laugh was kinda sexy, you ask me."

For all I knew, a high-pitched guy's voice might give the old man a hard-on. "Did you notice any strange noises before they left?"

"Before they left, I was asleep."

"Something woke you up?"

"Told you. Got up to take a whiz, like usual."

I wondered. What if a gunshot next door had awakened him? A gunshot could sound like a car backfiring. Late at night, people would be asleep and wouldn't necessarily hear. In this neighborhood, even if they heard gunshots and knew they were gunshots, they wouldn't necessarily do anything about it.

"Did he have any other visitors?"

"Nah."

"Are you sure?"

"I was here all day. Yeah, I'm sure."

"Thanks so much for talking to me," I said. "I didn't catch your name."

He smiled, shook his head, and closed the door.

This put a new spin on things. Derry's witness must be another neighbor. I had a witness who could testify that Garvey was alive when Melanie left him.

I went down to the mailboxes. The one for the old man's apartment was marked with a skull decal. Cute. I know where you live, old man, I thought. I would tell Derry and Ray about him. I'd subpoena his ass, if necessary.

I left the apartment complex and backtracked to the main road. I was thinking about whether to check for Bruce at Aces High, when I heard a squeal of tires behind me. A quick look in my rearview mirror brought me an unwelcome sight. It was Stavos' Lincoln, picking up speed and heading for me.

Chapter TWENTY-THREE

Don't panic, I thought. Just the sight of the Lincoln made my hands shake. To steady them, I gripped the wheel. It was hard to keep my eyes focused on driving, and I had to remind myself to do that or I'd risk rear-ending someone.

I resisted the urge to duck down a side street in a lame attempt to evade them. That's probably what they wanted. Get me to a deserted spot, maybe force my car over to the side. Stick with the crowd. Look for a cop.

If I found a cop, what would I say? *Help me, officer, I'm being chased by the Mafia.* He'd never believe it. Anyhow, there's never a cop around when you need one, and today was no exception.

I glanced in the rearview mirror. Only one car separated me from the Lincoln. The dark windows made it impossible to see who was driving, but I was willing to bet it was Scarface.

A long line of cars passed in the middle lane. On impulse, I swerved into the line in a masterful feat of precision driving and rudeness.

Almost immediately, the Lincoln flashed its turn signal. As it tried to move into my lane, horns honked and the car jerked back to the right. Eventually, it edged its way over, then moved to the extreme left lane and accelerated to catch up with me. It was doing a fine job, too. That was a car that got regular tune-ups.

I waited until it was close, then ducked back into the right lane. Within seconds, my old spot closed up, putting a line of cars between me and the Lincoln.

Up ahead, a light turned yellow. I hit the gas, determined to get through. So did the Lincoln's driver. The line of cars between us broke apart.

The Lincoln fell back, jockeying to get around the end of the line and fall in behind me again. If I stayed in the right lane, I'd eventually be dumped onto Route 1, and I didn't want that. I wanted to get to the interstate. You could always find a state cop there, patrolling for speeders. At the first small break, I pulled into the middle lane again. This drew an exasperated look from the guy behind me. I couldn't blame him.

The Lincoln's driver was starting to freak now, speeding up and slowing down, trying to figure out where he should be. I pictured Scarface pounding the wheel and calling me all kinds of names.

The Lincoln found a break in the traffic and got behind me again. But a pickup pulled between me and the Lincoln. Good. These guys probably wouldn't risk shooting strangers to get me. I figured the Mob was a bit more discreet than that. But if they got a clear shot, who knew what they'd do?

Another light turned yellow ahead, a major intersection. Again, I went for it, barely making it through. The pickup slowed to stop. Scarface hit the horn. The Lincoln swerved and, at the last moment, shot around the pickup and blew the red light. Fortunately, no one had moved off the line. Red light runners are so common around here, most sane people wait a few seconds after the light turns green.

Route 1 was ahead, which gave me two lights to get through—one for the northbound lanes, one for southbound, with a mini-block of developed median in between. If I could make it through those and a couple more, I could hit I-95, maybe even lose them.

The light changed as I sped down the hill. Before reaching the intersection, I punched it. About halfway through, I could see the light turn red. I checked the Lincoln.

Cars were inching forward as Scarface ran the light. The second light was yellow. I kept going. Then red. I went through anyway, with one open lane and something big coming. Christ, I thought, that was close. I glanced back.

The Lincoln barreled on. Crossing traffic began to move. Scarface honked again as he blew another red light.

I heard squealing tires, horns, then an explosive crash of metal hitting metal and shattering glass.

I found a place to pull off the road and walked back. The intersection was a mess. Several people had stopped and a few were talking on cell phones. The 911 lines had to be burning up.

A panel truck had T-boned the Lincoln, sending it sideways into a phone pole. The car sat atilt, wedged between the truck and the pole with its left wheels off the ground, trapping whoever was in the front seat. I moved in for a better view, trying to stick with the crowd as much as possible. Even from a distance, I could smell hot oil and burnt rubber. The truck driver was slumped over the wheel.

Within minutes, a fire truck, an ambulance, and a couple of cops were there. I hung back and watched the uniformed contingent moving with quick assurance through its paces. The cops set up flares and directed traffic. The rescue crew huddled around the vehicles. I waited and watched.

By the time they pulled Scarface from the Lincoln, he had a bandaged head, wore a neck brace, and rode a backboard. He was unconscious. If there's a God, I thought, let that bastard die.

A cop was talking to people on the corner. Witnesses, presumably. As the only person in the immediate area who really knew what the hell had happened, I guessed it was time to tell my story.

After talking to the cops, I went to the motel and got my things. I was willing to eat the cost of the room for that night, if necessary. Suddenly, the motel didn't seem all that nice. I didn't feel like spending the night in a room decorated by hospitality consultants. I wanted to go home and sleep in my own bed. I wanted to see my cat. Stavos had other things on his mind now. I didn't think he'd bother with me, at least not anytime soon.

I treated myself to dinner at my favorite Chinese restaurant—cashew chicken with fried rice and egg rolls. My fortune cookie read: *You will inherit a large sum of money*. I just hoped it would happen before this case killed me.

φ φ φ

The next morning, I lay half-awake in bed, mustering the effort to open my eyes when the phone rang. Blindly, I lunged over and picked it up.

"Hello?" It was my first-word-of-the-morning voice, sounding unused as an old garden gate and just as rusty.

"Sam?" It was Reed Duvall.

"Hi."

"Sorry. Did I wake you?"

"Naw. You just caught me in the middle of sanding my throat." I glanced at the clock radio. It was almost ten.

"You must be some crack investigator," I said. "'Cause I'm unlisted and I've never given you my number."

"Got it from Jamila."

"Ah, Jamila."

"I've been doing some research. Jamila said it was OK to share this new information."

"About what?"

"Connie Ash."

"Connie Ash? And?"

"And he's part of the case now. Along with the IRS."

"IRS?" I was beginning to feel like a parrot. "Is this going somewhere?"

"There's more. Why don't we meet somewhere?"

"You couldn't just tell me now?"

"I could, but let's meet. Feel like breakfast?"

"I could go for some food."

"Silver Diner? In about an hour?"

"Make it two, OK? I need a shower."

"Tell me you don't take showers that long."

"I don't. It's going to take me an hour and a half to crowbar myself out of bed."

"Here's an added incentive. I don't know all the details, but it seems to involve tax fraud."

Chapter TWENTY-FOUR

For the second time in two days, I had breakfast at a diner. This one was part of a chain. Like Frank's, Silver Diner had tabletop jukeboxes and Formica-and-stainless-steel decor, but the help consisted more of college students on summer break than professional wait staff. It was one of those nouveau diners, where meatloaf and mashed potatoes shared space on the menu with mesquite and lime marinated grilled salmon.

The line was out the door, so we snagged a couple of stools at the counter with its up-close view of the kitchen. Over the shelf where orders appeared for pickup, you could see a line of men in white, exchanging brief remarks in Spanish as they shoved more plates under the heat lamps. I inhaled the wonderful smell of bacon and eggs sizzling on the grill.

After we got coffee, Duvall said, "Your friend Christof Stavos has been in an accident."

"I know."

His eyebrows shot up. "Oh?"

I told him about my run-in with Stavos and associates. "I hope that wasn't part of your big news."

"No, no, no. Just leading up to it. My PGPD connection told me about the accident, so I went to the hospital. Looked like a cops convention."

"I thought only Jergins was interested in Stavos."

A waiter scurried by with eggs over easy in one hand and creamed chipped beef on toast in the other. Some traditions die hard, even in a nouveau diner.

"Well, they changed their minds or maybe they just wanted to keep an eye on Jergins. I don't know, but everyone was there—the Secret Service, Derry ..."

A waitress took our orders with a quick, practiced hand. She snapped the order form off the pad, pushed it across the shelf, then made a beeline to the coffeepots.

"I tried to sit in on the interrogation," Duvall said. "But someone spotted me, and they kicked me out."

"That wasn't very hospitable."

"No. I didn't miss much though. They took all of five minutes."

"Stavos probably insisted on having a lawyer present."

"That, plus the nurse insisted that they only take five minutes. From the looks of this nurse, I would have made it four-and-a-half."

"And?"

"And what?"

"I don't know. You're telling the story, and I still haven't heard anything about Ash and the IRS."

"I'm getting there. I don't know what they asked Stavos, but I know Jergins' concern in this case is finding Gregory Knudsen. It has something to do with a disc Stavos is looking for."

"I know about the disc. Stavos thought Melanie or I might have it."

"Jergins wants it, too."

"And?"

Duvall shot me a glance as he took a long sip of coffee. "And ... now the other cops are interested in Knudsen, too. Including the IRS."

"IRS agents were at the hospital?"

Duvall nodded. "There was one in the room when they questioned Stavos. Along with Jergins, some other FBI agent, the Secret Service, and Derry."

"You're sure he was an IRS agent?"

"That's what my friend says, and I have no reason to think he lied."

"What the hell would a tax collector be doing there?" I asked. "And what does Ash have to do with this?"

"Some kind of screw-up with his contracting, I heard. Something about a 1099. My friend isn't privy to all the info, but that's the rumor."

"Maybe it's not important to the investigation, if your friend doesn't know for sure."

"My friend isn't a detective. He just passes along what he hears."

"Maybe your friend was misinformed."

"Anything's possible."

"A 1099 is an income reporting form. I'm trying to picture how this would pertain to a murder investigation." I stopped, a thought forming. "Unless it relates to the identity theft case."

"Tax forms and identity. I can imagine a connection."

"But what is it?"

Our food came—a ham and cheddar omelet for me, a stack of pancakes for Duvall, with a side order of bacon to share. The waitress topped off our coffee.

Duvall picked up his cup and blew at the steam. "A lot of people who work at strip clubs are contractors."

"But how many of them are old friends with Bruce Schaeffer?"

"Garvey was a contractor," he said.

"Maybe this has something to do with the bookkeeping problems Rhonda Jacobi told me about. Maybe there was some kind of financial funny business going on and both Garvey and Schaeffer were involved."

"So where does Knudsen fit?"

"He knew Schaeffer. Schaeffer and Knudsen were friends in high school." I told him about my conversations with Bledsoe and Ferrengetti. "I don't know, but that woman, Barbara Ferrengetti, was screaming at Schaeffer about money and how Schaeffer was trying to protect Garvey. She had his child. Knudsen's child, that is."

"And Knudsen had mail coming to that P.O. Box."

"Right. And the key to the box was in Melanie's place, where Garvey used to live." I shook my head. "I just don't know. I can't keep it all straight."

"Schaeffer and Garvey and Knudsen."

"Oh, my."

"Wonder why that letter was in the box."

"Maybe that's where Knudsen sent the disc."

"But then the police should have found it."

I hesitated. "I guess."

"One more thing."

"What's that?"

"There were two other guys in the car with Stavos," Duvall said. "One of them was a rubber room candidate from the Bronx named Nicky Koutras. I say *was* because there's no Nicky Koutras anymore. He and the other guy in the front seat bought it."

I felt myself exhale, my shoulders relaxing as if they'd been carrying a weight for the past couple of weeks. "Did this Nicky Koutras have a big scar on his face?"

"Yeah," Duvall said. "I thought you might like to know."

ϕ ϕ ϕ

As we headed out to the parking lot, Duvall said, "So what're you up to on this fine Sunday?"

"I'm going to see Schaeffer. He won't want to talk to me, but I'm past the point of caring. Maybe he knows something about Knudsen."

"Think he's going to tell you, if he does?"

"Probably not, but if I don't try, I'll never know."

"Mind if I tag along?"

"Sure," I said. "Any particular reason?"

"If he was involved in the identity thefts, I'd like to know, too. Which reminds me—" Duvall gestured for me to follow him to his car. "I wanted to give you one of these." He opened the passenger door and retrieved a manila folder from which he pulled a piece of paper.

"I managed to dig this up," he said, handing it to me. "Thought it might come in handy, so I made a few copies."

It was Gregory Knudsen's old Maryland driver's license. He was a real cutie, all right. Brown, wavy hair, cut full on top and long in the back. A 1980s-style mullet that would have been popular around the time the license expired. His face was a display of all-American features, a regular boy-next-door look, well-proportioned, with a broad, nonthreatening smile. The effect was disarming, even from a grainy, blown-up copy of a thumbnail-sized photo.

"It's old, but someone might recognize him," Duvall said.

"Thanks." I kept examining the picture. There was something familiar about the face. Then I remembered Barbara Ferrengetti's son. He looked almost exactly like his dad. A daily reminder of the past. That had to hurt Barbara.

Chapter TWENTY-FIVE

Duvall followed me in his car to Schaeffer's place. I wondered if having Duvall with me would help or hurt. Would Schaeffer be less inclined to slam the door in the faces of two people who wanted to talk to him, or would he have twice as many reasons?

As Duvall held the vestibule door for me, I said, "What would you think of starting off the questioning? Last time I spoke to him, he walked away. I think being Melanie's attorney didn't help me much."

"Don't know if I'll do much better, but I'm willing to try."

"You're a guy. He'll relate better to you."

"Sure, all us guys relate so well."

"Well, at least you're not representing the woman he thinks killed his friend. Or so he says."

"True. I'll start, and you jump in whenever you feel like it."

"Assuming he bothers to answer the door," I said.

To my surprise, Schaeffer did answer the door. His hair looked wet, as if he'd just gotten out of the shower. I tried to get a peek into the place, to see if he had any fancy electronic gadgets like Barbara's, but Schaeffer leaned into the doorway, blocking most of my view. From what little I saw, the apartment wouldn't win any home decorating awards. If he had lots of money, he wasn't spending it on furniture.

Duvall introduced himself. "I think you've already met Ms. McRae."

Schaeffer's glance slid my way. He pulled himself up to full height. "Yeah."

"We're looking for someone you used to know," Duvall said. "Gregory Knudsen."

"What about him?"

"I said we're looking for him."

"Well, he ain't here."

"When was the last time you spoke to him?"

"I don't know," he said, in a gruff voice. "Years ago."

"You haven't seen or heard from him since he left Maryland?"

Schaeffer directed a level gaze at Duvall. "No."

"Did Tom ever mention him?" I asked.

"Why would he?" he said, without looking at me.

"I just thought Tom might have mentioned something about him and a certain disc."

One corner of his lip curled in a condescending smile. "I have no idea what you're talking about."

"Really? Because I understand that Tom and Gregory were blackmailing the Mob."

"The police have the Mob guy in custody," Duvall said. "We know Knudsen worked for him. We also know he was coming after your friend, Garvey. Apparently, there's a disc involved. And you're telling us you know nothing about that?"

"Why not just admit it," I said. "They knew each other. How?"

Schaeffer looked uncertain. "I don't know."

"So you're admitting they knew each other, but you don't know how?"

"I never said that," he said, raising his voice. "If they knew each other, I don't know about it."

"You didn't know Garvey in high school?"

"No."

"How did you meet him?"

Schaeffer worked his mouth. "On the job. He was a consultant where I work."

"At Aces High? You helped him get that job." I shook my head. "My understanding is you're old friends. When did you meet?"

He glared at me, his face growing red. "What the hell does it matter?"

"I don't know. I don't know if it matters that Knudsen's been getting mail at a P.O. Box in College Park. I guess it means he must be back in Maryland."

"Goody for him."

"The cops found the box key in Melanie's apartment," I said. "So ask her about it."

"I did. She doesn't know anything."

"What'd you think she'd say?"

"But why should she know him?" I paused a beat. "On the other hand, we've established that Garvey and Knudsen knew each other. The cops want to find Knudsen, and they'll probably want to talk to you about that."

Schaeffer looked haughty. "Fine. If the cops want me, they know where to find me." He looked ready to close the door.

"They might be interested in knowing about that list of social security numbers on your desk at work," I said, in a desperate attempt to keep the conversation going. "And those statements from First Bank."

Schaeffer looked like he'd been punched in the gut. The color drained from his face. His jaw went slack, and he gasped. "I don't know what you mean."

"Maybe Connie Ash could tell me more about them. His name was on the statements."

Schaeffer swallowed, trying to recover his composure. "You're lying. No way. You're lying."

"Your reaction suggests otherwise."

He drew himself up again, rebuilding his strength. "Fuck you. Fuck off." He slammed the door.

Duvall and I looked at each other. As we headed to the parking lot, he said, "Now, that's one guilty son of a bitch."

"Yeah, but guilty of what? Of knowing Gregory Knudsen? Big deal."

"What about those papers? You saw the way he acted."

"Sure, but where are they now? We still have no proof he was involved."

"The bank keeps those records, too. At least they'll have the bank statements."

"Schaeffer's name wasn't on them," I said. "But Ash's name was."

Duvall waited as I got in my car. The top was down, which was fine on a sunny, summer day except I wore shorts. As I slid in, the seat practically seared my bare thighs.

"I'd been thinking Schaeffer and Garvey might have stolen information from Ash's databases," I said. "What if Ash were in on it? What if he used Schaeffer and Garvey to steal the money, then stole it from them?"

"How do you figure?"

"Those bank statements had Ash's name on them. Maybe the money in those accounts is the money Schaeffer and Garvey stole."

"Motive?" Duvall asked.

"I don't know. He had tax problems. Maybe he needed to come up with ready cash."

"Why didn't he put another name on the accounts? Having the accounts in the club's name doesn't hide the money very well."

"True, unless Schaeffer and Garvey didn't know about those accounts," I explained.

"Curiouser and curiouser," Duvall said. "Jamila may want to subpoena Ash's bank records. Maybe depose Ash and Schaeffer."

"If she doesn't, I will." Tentatively, I leaned back against the hot seat. An asbestos seat cover would have come in handy.

"Might be worth looking into Ash's problems with the IRS," Duvall said.

"Might be."

"Of course, none of this will be necessary if the bank settles. They might do so to avoid the publicity of a trial."

"I wouldn't mind that. I'd rather focus on the murder charge. Speaking of which, I also found out yesterday from one of Schaeffer's neighbors that Tom Garvey was alive after Melanie saw him the weekend he died. He had other visitors very late Saturday night."

"Maybe this is your lucky weekend."

I started the car. "I hope so."

φ φ φ

I went home and called Melanie with the news about Stavos and Scarface. She was glad to hear she could move home.

"Karen has a one-bedroom, and I've been using her sofa," she said. "She's been very nice about it."

"There's more. Mostly good news, I think. You want to meet for dinner? We can celebrate your first night out of hiding."

"I could use a night out. OK."

We met at a Mexican restaurant in College Park, a mock adobe and tiled-floor simulation of a California mission and a popular hangout for the university crowd.

I gave Melanie a quick update on what I'd learned over the weekend. After our margaritas arrived, I raised my glass. "Here's to success in the future. When I clear you in this case, we can come back and really party."

Melanie lifted her glass with a whimsical look. "Here's to getting blasted." She took a drink, then added, "And forgetting about everything that's gone before. God knows, I've made enough mistakes."

"We all make mistakes."

"We don't all end up involved with criminals. Tom was good at keeping secrets. I never questioned the money he made at first. When the debts started to pile up, I wondered, but I guess I was blinded by some sort of hope he would work out."

"There are still a lot of unanswered questions. Like where is Gregory Knudsen and how does he fit in all this? You're sure you never heard of him?"

"Positive."

"He seems to have some connection to the Mob and the identity thefts. And supposedly, he knew Tom Garvey. He was supposed to have given him the disc."

"Tom didn't say anything about that. He said he had the disc, but that's all."

I pulled the photo Duvall gave me from my purse and unfolded it on the table. "This is a picture of Gregory Knudsen," I said, pointing to it. "Have you ever seen him?"

Melanie scrutinized the photo. "Huh."

"What is it?"

Her eyes widened and her mouth dropped open.

"Oh, my God." Her voice was faint.

"Do you know him?"

"He's younger and the hair is different, but that's his face." She pushed the paper toward me. "That's Tom."

Chapter TWENTY-SIX

"Are you sure?" I said.

"I'm positive." Melanie looked like she'd seen a ghost.

I realized then I'd never met Tom Garvey. He hadn't shown up in court for the protective order hearing. I had no reason to recognize him.

"If the cops are still looking for Knudsen, they must not know he's dead," I said.

"But if he assumed another name, wouldn't they find out?" Melanie asked.

"I don't know," I said. "If all his identification were in the name Tom Garvey, and Bruce identified him, why would they question it?"

"What about relatives? Wouldn't they need to notify someone?"

"Duvall said he had no next of kin."

Melanie shook her head. "I don't believe this."

"I better let Derry know," I said, digging for my cell.

I called Derry, Ray, and Reed Duvall. No one answered, so I left messages.

Ferrengetti also had to know that Knudsen and Garvey were the same. When she spoke to Schaeffer at the gym, she'd acted upset that Garvey was dead. Why would she be upset that the man who got her pregnant and left her was dead? Maybe she still loved him—or maybe something else was going on. Something that involved money. And Schaeffer.

You can change your name, I thought, but you can't change your past. No matter how far you run, it always seems to catch up with you. Something had caught up with Gregory Knudsen, a.k.a. Tom Garvey. Maybe understanding that was the key to finding his killer.

φ φ φ

I slept in the next day and felt a lot better for it. It was going to take time for me to recover from my all-night escapade at Aces High, but I felt like I was three-quarters of the way there. I was supposed to relax, but I hadn't had a relaxed moment since leaving the hospital. I couldn't believe it had been less than a week.

After breakfast, I looked over the notes from my various interviews. Rhonda had mentioned the books were weird. Could it have been for reasons other than Bruce's bad bookkeeping? Assuming Ash was more involved with his businesses than everyone thought, he'd been lying to me. But why then would he put his own name on those bank accounts?

I could press Rhonda for more details about Ash. It was too early for the club to be open, so I went online and found a listing for R. Jacobi. She lived in Laurel, not far from Bruce Schaeffer.

I dialed the number and got a machine. Rhonda's gravelly voice came over the line.

"Hi. I can't get to the phone right now …"

I tuned out the rest of the message. The beep brought me around, and I stammered out my name and "please call me," or words to that effect.

I hung up and replayed Rhonda's recorded greeting in my head. It was the way she said "phone." I hadn't noticed before, but she had that Baltimore accent, same as Ferrengetti. Was it a coincidence she worked with Schaeffer and lived close to him?

Lots of people from Baltimore move to Laurel. It didn't
necessarily mean anything.

I couldn't be sure about Jacobi, but I knew Ferrengetti lied to
me. It was time to confront her. On the way, I could swing by
the club, just in case Rhonda had gone in early.

φ φ φ

The place looked different. Could have been the cop cars in the
parking lot and the crime scene tape strung everywhere.

I banged on the door for a bit before Derry answered.

"Hi," I said. "There can't be a good reason for this." I waved
my hand at the tape.

"There very rarely is." He arched an eyebrow. "May I ask
what you're doing here?"

"I was hoping to talk to one of the assistant managers if she's
here."

"She's not, but someone else is. Bruce Schaeffer with half his
head blown off. Looks like suicide."

"Oh."

"You understand why I can't let you in."

"That's just fine," I said. I didn't need to see Schaeffer's
brains on a wall. "God, I just spoke to him yesterday. He wasn't
happy to talk to me, but I wouldn't have pegged him as
suicidal."

"Obviously, it's too early to say, but we're finding some
interesting things in here," Derry said. "The gun he used is the
same caliber used on Garvey. Or should I say Gregory
Knudsen?"

"You got my message."

"Yeah. Kind of supports the notion that Garvey—or
Knudsen—was involved in identity theft. We also found boxes
of files like the one in your client's apartment."

I stared at him. "Really? What's in them exactly?"

"Don't know. I'm handling the homicide part of this.
Someone else will have to take a look after we bring them in."

"A lot of boxes?"

"At least five or six so far."

I tried not to look as stunned as I felt. If those boxes had been there two nights ago, Duvall and I would have seen them.

"Who found him?"

"Custodian. In the office."

I shook my head. "Looks like there's a job opening at Aces High."

"Mmm." Derry's mustache twitched in response.

"Does Agent Jergins know about Knudsen yet?"

"I left a message this morning. He's not going to like it." I swear Derry grinned.

"What's the deal with him, anyway? Why's he so interested in Knudsen?"

Derry paused, then shrugged, as if he couldn't think of a good reason not to tell me. "Stavos and his minions were skimming money from the big bosses. Knudsen overheard them and recorded their conversations. He blackmailed Stavos, but had to hit the road when Stavos figured out who was doing it. He burned the conversations on a CD, which he must have brought with him to Maryland."

"And Knudsen changed his name to protect himself from Stavos," I said.

"Probably. Of course, try hiding from organized crime. It's not all that easy to just disappear. I guess when the heat started to come down on Knudsen, he must have turned to the FBI. By that time, he'd changed his name. Jergins was assigned the case, but never had a chance to meet Garvey, or the man he thought of as Garvey, who was supposed to have a disc Knudsen gave him. When we didn't find the disc at the murder scene, Jergins figured Knudsen had it."

"Why is Jergins so interested? Is the disc evidence in a prosecution?"

"No. As I understand it, Jergins wanted to use the information to force Stavos to rat on the Mob."

"I see. Either cooperate with the feds, or they'd send the information to Stavos' big boss."

"In which case, Mr. Stavos would become history," Derry said.

Cute. A blackmailer for greed turning evidence over to a blackmailer for justice. One had to admire the symmetry.

After I left Aces High, I took another detour toward Gibson Island.

With the wind ruffling my short hair, I raced down the road, singing a high-pitched tune over the roar of my car's motor. The air was damp and close, and at sixty miles an hour, it slapped at me like a moist towel.

I wondered about Ash. Could he have used Knudsen and Schaeffer to steal the money, then killed them? He could have planted those files to make them look guilty. But why would he set up Melanie?

What about Ash's tax problems? Maybe the situation with Garvey's 1099 had something to do with him not really being Garvey. Maybe *Ash* was a victim here. If I asked him a few more questions, the worst he could do was tell me to pound sand. Well, maybe it wasn't the worst he could do. Thing was, even though Ash struck me as indolent, rich, and irresponsible, I couldn't imagine him killing anyone.

A blue line of water appeared in the distance, with the Gibson Island guard station looming in the foreground. I was thinking up an excuse for the guard, when I noticed a silver Lexus racing off the island. Ash's car. It flew by me in a silver blur.

I found a place to turn around and followed him.

Chapter TWENTY-SEVEN

Ash was out of sight. I put my foot to the floor. The wind roared, as the speedometer needle passed eighty, inching toward eighty-five. I was getting every penny's worth of the work that had gone into fixing my car. The old heap actually had a lot of giddyup. I swore to maintain the thing religiously from then on.

The silver Lexus gleamed in the distance, moving into the right lane and signaling to get off at the Baltimore-Washington Parkway. I followed, pushing it on the turn, my tires kicking up dust as they hit the dirt shoulder. He had a good lead on me, but parkway traffic was light. I mashed the pedal again.

Ash got off at the exit for Baltimore-Washington International Airport. I followed him past the hotels and down a side road toward long-term parking. As he entered the lot, I pulled over and watched him park. He got out and hauled a large suitcase and a shoulder bag from the trunk, then strode toward a bus shelter. A shuttle bus circling through the lot stopped at the shelter, and he got on. The bus rolled off toward the terminal. So much, I thought, for that.

I found a pay phone off the parkway and called the PG police. I was starting to feel like one of their operatives. Derry wasn't back, so I left a message about Ash. The rest was up to him.

Maybe Ash planned to leave town all along. Maybe not. One way or the other, I couldn't do a thing about it.

φ φ φ

Barbara answered the door in pajama pants and a cropped white T-shirt. I could hear the TV in the background. One of those morning talk shows where cheating boyfriends and drug-addicted daughters come to confess their sins before an audience clapping like trained seals.

"What do you want now?" she said.

"Why didn't you tell me Greg Knudsen and Tom Garvey were the same person?"

She smiled. "So what about it?"

"So it's quite an oversight."

"I don't have to talk to you." She started to close the door.

"It's either me or the cops."

She held up, squinting at me. "Whadda you mean?"

"They might be interested in hearing about your argument at the gym with Bruce Schaeffer. They might like to know about your financial situation since Knudsen, the prodigal father, came back to town."

"Prod-*what?*"

"Bruce Schaeffer's been shot."

Her mouth fell open and her face went white.

"If I go to the police and tell them about your argument, they could get very interested in you."

Barbara's jaw flapped a bit. "So I had an argument with Bruce. That don't mean I killed him."

"Maybe. Maybe not. It could mean you were involved in the identity theft scheme with him."

"What're you—"

"Don't bother to deny it. The cops found the evidence. And I don't think you bought your nice new SUV and your nice new TV with what you get milking the workers' comp office."

She didn't say anything, but I could see the wheels turning in her head. "What do you want?"

"I want the whole story. I want to know how you got involved and what your part was."

She looked resigned, but shoved the door farther open. I took that as a tacit invitation to come in and followed her to the living room. The talk show was blasting through the fancy sound system. A bowl of melting ice cream sat on the coffee table. My eye strayed to Mahogany Jesus on the wall. He seemed particularly forlorn.

Barbara plunked onto the sofa and muted the TV. Under the cropped top, I could see a little tummy roll. She was a thin woman, but was going to learn the hard way that metabolism slows with age.

"I wasn't involved. I swear, I wasn't."

"So how did you come into all this extra money? Or are you overextending your credit to buy all this shit?"

"I didn't steal, OK? He owed me."

"You're talking about Knudsen now?"

She nodded.

"He would have owed you a bundle in child support after all those years."

"Fifteen years." Her face was livid. "I told him, I'd take him to court. The little shit owed me thousands of dollars."

"Tens of thousands, quite likely. More than he could have paid you."

"Yeah, well." She paused, shifting around. "We made a deal."

"What kind of deal?"

"To keep it out of court, he cut me in on the scam."

"Scam? You mean the identity thefts?"

"Yeah, whatever. Bruce didn't like it much, but Greg said too bad. Suddenly, the cocksucker couldn't do enough for me." Her voice became a derisive whine. "Goddamn son of a bitch. All those years, he could have sent me some money, just a little. But no. I raised his bastard son single-handed. He couldn't even be bothered to see him."

"Did Melanie figure in this?"

"Melanie?"

"Tom's girlfriend. I mean, Greg's. You know what I mean."

"Oh, her. I don't think that poor, dumb slut had a clue."

"So she wasn't involved?"

"Not as far as I know. It was just Greg and Bruce."

"What about Connie Ash?"

"Who's she?"

"He. Conrad Ash is the club owner."

She shook her head. "Never even heard of her. Him. Whatever."

"All right," I said. "So you blackmailed Greg into paying you part of what they stole. And after he was killed, I guess you had enough on Bruce to keep soaking him."

"Well, why not? Hey, I told you. Greg owed me. When he died, he still owed me. If he'd been any sort of man, he'd have married me, made his bastard son legit. Instead, he skulks back to Maryland and takes up with some slut."

I peered at her. "Why do you keep calling Melanie a slut?"

"He was spending money on her that he should have given me. She was living in sin with him."

I laughed. "And you had his illegitimate child, Snow White."

"If he'd married me fifteen years ago, that wouldn't be the case."

I decided not to delve into the twisted logic that a religious fanatic might use to purify "dirty" premarital sex with a post factum marriage.

"Even if you don't believe in abortion, you could have given the child up for adoption."

"Damn straight, I don't believe in abortion. And, yeah, I could have given the kid away, but I didn't." She stabbed a finger at her chest. "*I* did the right thing."

Whatever, I thought. "Who do you think killed Gregory Knudsen?"

She shrugged. "I don't know."

"With Greg out of the picture, maybe you thought you could force Bruce to pay more."

Barbara looked shocked. "You're not saying I killed him, are you? He was the whole reason I was getting a cut to begin with."

"But by that time, you knew about the scheme. Maybe you threatened to go to the cops, to put the screws on Bruce."

"Why the hell would I kill Greg?"

"I don't know. It's a crime of passion. You hated Greg Knudsen. How many more reasons would you need?"

She made a sputtering noise between pursed lips. I took it to mean she disagreed with my theory.

"What about the files in Melanie's apartment? Did you put them there?"

"Files?"

"Files of the various accounts they set up using the stolen identities."

"Oh, those. Bruce had the files. I didn't have nothing to do with them."

"So he set her up?"

"He must've. He was nervous about Greg's body being in his apartment. He moved the shit out before calling the cops, 'cause he figured they'd search the place."

"So why'd he hold onto the files?"

"I wanted to know what they were raking in. Bruce was supposed to destroy them after that."

"And everything was fine, until Greg was murdered?"

She paused. "Well ..."

"Yes?"

Barbara hesitated again, looking wary. "I don't know. Not long after I got in on it, Greg told me someone else took the money."

"Huh?"

"He was probably lying. He said it was in some bank account and someone took it out. Now how can that be?"

I thought about the bank statements I'd seen at Aces High. I remembered the stricken look on Bruce's face when I mentioned them.

"So he said he couldn't pay me so much," Barbara went on. "I made a big stink about it, but he said it was for real."

"Someone stole the money that they stole?"

"Hey, I'm telling you what he said. I'm not saying I believe it. Greg kept paying me something. After he died, Bruce wouldn't pay at first, but I got him to change his mind."

"By threatening to go the cops? Were you arguing about that at the gym?"

Her face hardened into a resolute look. "They owed me."

I sighed. "Well, it's over now. Bruce is dead."

Barbara slumped. "Great. Fucking great."

"Yeah. I'll let you mourn in peace." I rose and started for the door, then stopped. "Oh, one more thing. How did you find out that Greg Knudsen was back?"

Barbara stared straight ahead. "Someone called and told me," she said in a flat voice.

"Who?"

"I dunno. They didn't give a name."

"Man or woman?"

"Could've been either."

"You have caller ID?"

Barbara shut her eyes and took a deep breath. "No-o-o."

"Would you have a guess who it was?"

"No, and I couldn't care less, in case you hadn't noticed."

"Actually, I did notice."

I walked out, leaving Barbara with her bowl of ice cream soup and her problems.

Chapter TWENTY-EIGHT

The hot afternoon sun had turned the sky to a gray haze stew. In a nearby park, trees undulated and bowed restlessly in the fitful breeze, the silky shoosh of their leaves sounding like distant applause from an outdoor amphitheater. As I waited at a red light, I could almost smell the rain on the verge of dropping from the clouds.

Who would have ratted Knudsen out? And why?

You can run from the past, but it always catches up with you. Had someone from Knudsen's past caught up with him? Ryan Bledsoe might know, but he was in Ocean City by now.

I could think of people I hated in high school—if I really gave it some thought. I could hardly remember most of them now. If someone from Knudsen's past had it in for him, he must have done something dreadful—something a person would remember fifteen or twenty years later.

The light changed. Instead of going straight to I-95, however, I asked the first passerby I saw the way to Dundalk High School.

I pulled into the school's lot and parked next to the low, flat building. Strolling the quiet, locker-lined halls, I flashed back to a time when a place like this was my universe—a place where cliques ruled and some scowling academic was either threatening to fail you or put a black mark on your permanent record.

I got good grades and never had a smudge, as far as I knew, on that much-storied record, but the high school experience was a far from satisfactory one for me. My memory was of social circles—jocks, scholars, nerds, freaks. Then there was that special group—the ruling elite. The ones who ran for student council or edited the yearbook. The ones who always had the right clothes or just seemed to have a special aura. I was at the other end of the social spectrum—one of the kids so far out of the loop, we didn't merit a special category. I wondered where they were now, those kids who peaked in high school. Probably fat, alcoholic, and either unhappily married or miserably alone—at least, I wanted to think so.

No one was behind the counter in the administrative office. A desk on the other side had a nameplate reading, Ida Wilkie, but Ida herself was not present. Then a petite, middle-aged woman appeared with several files on one arm. The woman had a broad, florid face, pert nose, and short hair, just a trifle too dark and monochromatic to be her real color. She beamed at me, as if glad for the interruption.

"Can I help you?" she said, setting the files on her desk.

"I hope so. My name's Sam McRae. I'm an attorney, representing someone in a case involving two guys who were students here. I don't know if you would know them. It was over fifteen years ago."

"I was here."

"The names are Gregory Knudsen and Bruce Schaeffer."

"Oh." Her eyes widened and the shadow of some emotion I couldn't identify crossed her face.

"You recognize the names?"

"Yes, I do. And you're a lawyer, you said? What did you say this was about?"

"Gregory Knudsen was murdered a few weeks ago. Just this morning, Bruce Schaeffer was also found dead."

She looked grim. "Murdered?"

"It looks like suicide, but I have my doubts."

"Who are you representing?"

"The person accused of Knudsen's murder."

Ida didn't say anything. She didn't look quite as happy to talk to me.

"My client is innocent. I have a witness who can establish that. She was set up, possibly by someone those guys knew in high school. That person may have killed both of them."

"Why would it be another student from this school?"

"I'm not sure. I know that Greg Knudsen left Maryland about fifteen years ago and came back recently. And from what I understand, Knudsen and Schaeffer were troublemakers in high school."

Ida lifted an eyebrow. "I can't talk about their disciplinary records, you know."

"I'm not as interested in that as in finding out who their enemies were."

"Oh, they had plenty."

"Can you remember who? It's been a long time, and I realize you probably aren't that close to the students."

"You'd be surprised." She gave me a wry smile. "They talk to me sometimes. Especially the troubled ones, who end up in there." She jerked a thumb over her shoulder, toward what I assumed was the principal's office. "Seems like we're getting more of those."

"You'd remember stuff from fifteen years ago?"

She tapped her temple with an index finger. "I remember everything. My friends say I have total recall. I don't know. But I remember lots of things, and I've been here thirty-five years. Can you believe it?"

I peered at her. I realized she must be quite a bit older than she looked, maybe her late sixties. "Well, no, actually. You don't look a day over forty—forty-five —tops."

She burst out laughing. "You're so sweet." She gave the word *so* that nasal Baltimore sound—*sohww.*

"Can you remember anyone in particular? An enemy or even a friend they might have double-crossed or something?"

One side of Ida's mouth quirked up, forming a parentheses mark on her cheek. "They were quite a pair. Frequent visitors here. Like I said, plenty of people had reason to dislike them."

"I spoke to someone who attended school around the same time. Ryan Bledsoe."

"Mmm-hmm."

"He told me they were expelled after a chemistry lab fire."

"I can't talk—"

"I know you can't talk about their records. Can you confirm a rumor? Was someone killed in that fire?"

She looked at me.

"Ryan Bledsoe told me they were expelled, and said there was a rumor that someone died in the fire. Is this true?"

She continued to look at me, her expression thoughtful. "No. But you're on the right track."

It took a moment for me to realize what she was saying. "Someone was hurt?"

She nodded.

"Badly?"

She nodded again.

"A student?"

More nodding. It felt like a game of twenty questions.

"What happened to the student?"

"She dropped out of school. Don't know what happened after that."

A girl, I thought. "I don't suppose you'd remember her name?"

Ida smiled. "I figured you might get around to that."

"Do you remember?"

"The mother sued the school. The case settled. The school board wanted to keep it quiet. Legally, I don't think anything prevents me from talking about it, but I've been, um, encouraged not to, in the interests of this person's privacy."

Or the school board's interest in sweeping the matter under the rug, I thought. "So you can't reveal the name?"

"I'd prefer not to."

"Even if this injured student might have killed two people?"

She didn't say anything.

I tried another tack. "This fire—it happened when Knudsen and Schaeffer were juniors?"

"Yes," she said, throwing aside all bureaucratic pretense of not discussing the matter.

"The student—also a junior?"

"Uh huh."

"I was wondering—do you have copies of the yearbooks for that time?"

Ida smiled. "Yes, in the library. I can get them for you." She fished a key ring from a drawer.

I tried to calculate which years I'd want. "I'd be interested in—"

"I think I know which ones." She left the office. She returned a few minutes later with two yearbooks, which she set on a round table in the corner. One would have been from the guys' junior year, the other from the year after.

I sat at the table. If my theory didn't pan out, this could take a while, and it would be tedious. I could check the junior class pictures in the earlier yearbook against the senior photos in the later yearbook and narrow the suspects down to a manageable set of names.

But I already had a theory about who it was. A girl with a Baltimore accent.

"Thanks," I said to Ida. I opened the book and went right to the *J*s in the junior class photos.

Ida stood and watched. Finally, she said, "You might try the *T*s," and walked away.

φ φ φ

Despite the different name, I recognized her. Just to be sure, I checked the senior photos for the following year. As I expected,

Rhonda Timson wasn't among them. Somewhere along the line, she must have married or changed her name. She was younger, thinner, and free of facial scars, but it was Rhonda Jacobi.

Chapter TWENTY-NINE

I called Duvall when I got home and left another message.

I had a message from Detective Derry, thanking me for the information about Ash. Unfortunately, he said, taking a trip by airplane was not grounds for arrest or even a search warrant in Maryland. Of course it wasn't. Just like working at a strip club with two guys who negligently disfigured you almost twenty years ago wasn't grounds either. Or living three blocks from one of them.

If it was a coincidence, it was a big one. Other things were making sense now, too. Rhonda could have set up the accounts. She could have taken the money. She had access to the information she needed.

I went online and looked up Skip Himmelfarb's phone number. He picked up on the second ring.

"Hey, Skip, it's Sam McRae," I said.

"Hi," he said, the surprise apparent in his voice.

"Look, I hope you don't mind my calling you at home, but I have a question about Rhonda."

"Oh?"

"Do you know how long she's worked at Aces High?"

"Hmm. I think she started a couple of months after me. Why?"

"Was this before or after Tom began there?"

"I'm not sure."

"Try to remember."

"I'm a bit vague on this, but I think it might have been after," he said.

"I have a kind of delicate question to ask. Has she ever talked about why her face is scarred?"

He hesitated. "Why do you ask?"

I felt embarrassed for bringing it up, but it seemed necessary. "I'm just curious."

"I think she said she was burned in a fire."

"I see. Did she mention when it happened and how? Was it in high school?"

"I don't know. What does this have to do with Tom's murder?"

"Nothing necessarily," I said. I wasn't going to speculate to Skip about my theories. "I appreciate the information. Thanks."

φ φ φ

Aces High was closed, cordoned off. The lot was empty. I turned around and headed toward Laurel.

Rhonda lived in the same apartment complex as Bruce. I checked the mailboxes for the unit number. It was down one flight.

I knocked on the door twice, but there was no answer, so I returned to the car.

Rhonda could have been at a day job. I checked my watch. It was around four o'clock. I hadn't had a thing to eat since breakfast and my stomach was growling. It could take Rhonda hours to come home. For all I knew, she might not return for a month. For all I knew, she might never come back.

I drove to the nearest Burger King in a strip shopping center with a CVS drugstore and a Giant grocery. After doing the drive-through, I tried to reach Reed Duvall on my cell, but my last bar winked out in mid-dial. In all the excitement, I'd forgotten to recharge the stupid thing. I found a pay phone, and called Duvall the old-fashioned way. Got the message machine again. He must have been working on something hot.

"Hey," I said, after the beep. "Where've you been all day? I went by Rhonda Jacobi's. She's not there. I might hang around her place a bit, see if she shows up. Call you when I get home."

I didn't know what else to do. Before going back to Rhonda's, I went into CVS and bought a paperback. This could take a while.

I backed into a space with a good view of her building. After knocking on her door again, I returned to the car, cracked my new book, and started to read.

They say surveillance is boring. They're right. Rhonda still wasn't there by five. People came home from work. I kept reading. Rhonda wasn't home by six either. People went out to dinner. Another hour crawled by. Still no sign of her.

I was glad to have the book, a mystery by someone named Walter Mosley. I don't read mysteries, but this one was pretty good. I read it fast. More people came and went. At eight, nothing had changed.

I read until the sun set, then I turned on the radio, keeping it low. The wind died and the car stayed hot. I was soaked in sweat, my shirt plastered to my back and the undersides of my thighs sliding on the Naugahyde seat. The smell of honeysuckle drifted through the window. An unseen horde of cicadas raised their cyclical buzz into the night sky, sounding like someone pedaling an old bicycle, faster and faster, until the tune reached a crescendo and died. The cicadas took a breather and launched into another rendition. I stopped counting the number of times they did this after six.

Lightning flashed, strobe-like, revealing the marbled pattern of cloud outlines. An angry rumble followed several seconds later. Everything else was still.

I'll give it another half hour, I thought.

About fifteen minutes later, she came home.

Headlight beams swept across the lot, then a small car pulled up near the building. Rhonda Jacobi got out and hurried inside. I switched off the radio and waited.

Within minutes, Rhonda came out, carrying a box. She shoved the box into the car and dashed back in the building. A few more minutes and she returned with another box. Into the car it went. I watched her do this a few more times. Sometimes it was boxes, sometimes a miscellaneous item or two—a broom, a mop, a torchiere lamp. Then she came out with a suitcase. She opened the trunk and heaved it in, then disappeared again. I didn't need to be Sherlock Holmes to figure it out.

It's now or never, I thought. When Rhonda reappeared with more bags, I left the car and walked toward her.

Chapter THIRTY

Rhonda leaned into the trunk, so intent on packing, she didn't notice me.

"Going somewhere?" I said.

She jerked upright and whirled around. "God, you scared me," she said, a little squeak creeping into her gravelly voice. "What are you doing here?"

"Looks like you're moving."

"Yeah."

"Why did you lie about Bruce and Tom? Or should I say, Bruce and Greg?"

The change in topic appeared to disorient her. "What do you mean?"

"You never told me you knew them in high school."

"I *didn't* know them."

"But you did know Tom Garvey was actually Greg Knudsen."

"So?"

"You knew they were responsible for the accident that scarred your face."

Rhonda's expression grew hard. "What about it?"

She didn't deny anything. That worried me.

"So why would you work with two people who did that to you?"

"I needed a job."

"You expect me to believe it was a complete coincidence, your taking that particular job?"

Rhonda leaned against the car and crossed her arms. "Why should I care what you believe?"

"You also knew who Barbara was, and why she was arguing with Bruce."

Thunder rumbled like distant tympani. Rhonda stared at me with an intense expression that belied her casual pose.

"Did you tell her Greg was back in town?" I said.

No response.

"Did you steal the money?"

Nothing.

"If they were using the club's accounts to hide the money they stole, you would have known it. You had access to the records."

Rhonda glanced at her fingernails as if bored. "I don't know what you're talking about."

"If you had access to the files, you must have put them in the office after you killed Bruce."

"Bruce killed himself."

"I don't believe it. Those files weren't there before."

"How do you know?"

"I just know."

"How will you prove it?"

I didn't say anything.

She smiled. "You see. You have nothing."

"The police will figure out soon enough that Bruce didn't kill himself."

"And if they do, so what?" Rhonda's voice was mocking.

I hadn't the slightest idea. "What I can't figure out is, why kill them?" I said. "You must have gone to a lot of trouble—gaining their confidence, stealing their money. You could have blackmailed them, and they couldn't have done anything about it. So why kill them?"

"You're grasping at straws, sweetie."

"Better question still, why set my client up for Knudsen's murder? Why divert suspicion from Bruce?"

For the first time, Rhonda reacted with something more than detached amusement or indifference. I thought I caught a flash of anger in her eyes. Maybe it was the lightning.

"Obviously, Bruce must've done it and set her up," she said.

"It's possible, but why didn't he just plant the gun in her apartment? Why set her up with a box of files that linked his crimes to the murder? In a box from Aces High, no less."

We stared at each other. The approaching storm boomed in the background, like an invading army. Now and then, a car went by, the driver oblivious to two women staring each other down.

"Bruce didn't have a motive," I said. "You did."

She looked away, her cheeks twitching.

"You resented Melanie. That's why you set her up."

"No." The directness of her response took me aback. "I wouldn't do that."

"But you would steal and kill."

Rhonda laughed, her mouth twisting into a sneer. "Why are you so concerned with those guys? They were shit. They deserved to die."

"I'm not concerned with them. I'm concerned with my client."

"She wasn't involved."

"Now it's my turn to ask, how do you know?"

"She's not the type."

"I thought you didn't know her."

"She was just another victim, OK?" She raked her hair back from her face, revealing a confused expression. "Another Greg Knudsen victim."

"I thought you didn't know him well."

"Everyone knew Greg was trouble. Him and Bruce."

"So she was a victim. Like Barbara? Like yourself?"

"Yes. We were all victims. And those bastards deserved what they got."

"And you made sure they got it."

"Give it a rest, OK? You have nothing."

"And you're counting on being gone by the time I have something."

Rhonda stood there, breathing heavily. Her face was moon-like in its pallor, and her eyes glittered. She pulled a crushed pack of Lucky Strikes from her purse—I couldn't help but notice the red bull's-eye on it—and tapped a cigarette out. Placing it between her lips, she dug through her bag until she found a lighter. It flared with a snap in her shaking hands.

"Skip," I said. "Did he—"

Before I could finish the thought, a car pulled up behind me. I turned. It was Skip behind the wheel of a white Chevy Cavalier. He held a handgun.

Chapter THIRTY-ONE

Skip unfolded himself from the car, pointing the gun at me. It pretty much answered the question I'd started to ask. He looked about as natural with a gun as I would have carrying a jackhammer.

He looked from me to Rhonda and back at me. "What's going on?"

"Put that away," Rhonda said.

Skip shook his head.

"What are you going to do with it?" Rhonda spoke as if to an unruly child.

"What's going on?" He repeated the words in a soft, throaty voice.

"I'm ready to go. Are you?" Rhonda said.

He nodded my way. "What does she know?"

"Nothing. Not a goddamn thing. Now shut your mouth."

"The cops came by my place."

Rhonda did a double take. "What? When?"

"Today. This afternoon."

"What'd you tell them?"

"I didn't answer the door. I heard them talking about getting a warrant."

"How the hell can they do that?"

"I don't know." He looked at me. "What do you know about this?"

"Nothing," I said in complete truth.

His gaze shifted to Rhonda.

"What?" she said.

"Did you tell them anything?"

Rhonda's jaw dropped. "Are you crazy?"

"Why would they be able to get a warrant?"

"I don't know. Don't look at me. I wouldn't … you *know* I wouldn't. Not after everything—"

She shot a nervous glance at me.

Skip appeared dazed. "After everything I've done for you?"

"That's enough," Rhonda said.

He didn't react to her words.

"What did you do?" I asked.

"Shut up!" Rhonda yelled.

I wasn't sure if she was talking to me or Skip.

"Nothing," he said. "Everything."

"What do you mean?"

"Skip, don't say another word."

"You killed them?" I said. "Why?"

"No," he said. "But I let it happen."

"Goddamn you." Rhonda's face was livid. "How can you do this to me?"

"I can't let it go on," he said.

"What?" I said. "Let what go on?"

"The lies. They'll come after us, you know. They'll come after me."

"Did you steal the money?" I asked, trying to make sense of his words.

"Yes. And that's all it was supposed to be. No one was supposed to get hurt."

I looked at Rhonda. Tears streamed down her face.

"Oh, you fool," she said. "I love you, but you're such a fool."

"All this time, I covered for you," he said. "I protected you. All because of an accident fifteen years ago. But I'm not going to prison, not even for you."

"We did the right thing," Rhonda said, her voice rising.

She looked at me. The tears made her face look like it was melting.

"I never meant to kill Greg. It wasn't supposed to happen," she said.

"But it did. And you set my client up."

"No. I did it for her."

I gaped at her. "What?"

"I did it for her and all the other women that man screwed over." She paused, sniffling. "Bruce was out of town. I took care of the club that weekend. Greg called me." She smiled bitterly. "I love this. He wanted to see me, 'cause he thought Bruce was ripping him off. Isn't that good? He thought I could help him prove Bruce used the business accounts to steal the money.

"He wouldn't leave his apartment, so I went to his place. He was acting all weird about something—said some crazy guy was after him. Anyway, I figured I'd play along, pretend I didn't know anything about the money. I was thinking maybe I could set Bruce up with Greg, and Greg with Bruce. Play one against the other."

She took a deep breath, exhaling a shuddering sigh. "Greg said he'd be up, so we went by after closing. He looked like hell. A regular Howard-fucking-Hughes. He looked like he hadn't slept in a while, and he smelled. No wonder he and Bruce weren't getting along. Anyway, before I could say anything, I noticed the papers. He'd left them on a table in the living room. Your name was on them."

"Papers?"

"The one's that said he'd beaten on your client."

"The petition for the protective order?"

She shook her head. "I guess so. Whatever they were, I just snapped when I saw them. After everything he'd done, now he was beating up on women. I just snapped. I took the gun from my purse and I shot him."

"You carry a gun?"

"I took it with me that night," Rhonda said. "It's a gun I keep at the club."

"I gave it to her for protection," Skip said. His voice sounded far off.

"And you were with her, at this meeting with Greg?" I asked.

"Yes," he said.

"Did you try to stop her from shooting him?"

He shook his head, looking at me as if he couldn't imagine why I'd ask such a thing.

"It was strange," Rhonda said. "I did it without thinking twice. And afterward, I didn't care. Why would I care about exterminating a bug?"

Skip looked at her, a trace of sadness in his eyes. "He wasn't a bug."

"He was evil," she hissed. "He deserved what he got and you know it."

"And Bruce?" I said.

"Bruce figured out I took the money. When you told him about the bank statements, he put it together. He had thought Greg was ripping him off, that Barbara was putting more pressure on him, making him pay more. It never occurred to him I'd be involved. The guy was so sloppy. You'd think he'd go the extra mile to throw out the evidence somewhere far away, but he just threw it in the club's Dumpster. I took it out and kept it.

"When he realized what was going on, he came to the club, all pissed off. He stormed into the office, grabbed me outta the chair, and threw me on the floor. Then he said if I didn't give back the money, he'd personally beat the crap out of me. He didn't hear Skip."

I looked at Skip who wouldn't look back.

"I knocked him out," he said. "Hit him over the head, with a fire extinguisher. We picked him up and moved him to the chair. I was still trying to figure out what we should do, when she …" His voice faded out.

"Why kill him?" I said to Rhonda.

"He deserved it."

"Why not go to the police? Did you want the money?"

"Hell, I didn't care about the money. Besides, what would happen if I told the cops? They'd give him probation, maybe order him to pay back what he took. A slap on the wrist, that's all he'd get. Just like when they blew up the lab. They could never be punished enough for what they did to me."

"What they did to you," I said. "That's what it comes down to. You wanted revenge."

Rhonda froze me with her stare. In the dark, her pupils were huge, her eyes glassy. "You make it sound so fucking simple. The legal system's a joke. The school paid my family off years ago, but I get to live with this." She placed a hand against her scarred cheek. "Well, it wasn't enough. So I created my own form of justice."

"If everyone did that, we'd have anarchy."

"I knew you wouldn't understand." She scowled in disapproval. "What do you know? You little fucking Girl Scout. You'll take money to be a mouthpiece, but what do you really do that solves problems? I took steps." Spit flew from her mouth. "I solved the problem."

She turned away. "We'll have to kill her," she said to Skip.

"No," he replied.

Rhonda started to say something, but stopped short, her eyes wide. Skip was pointing the gun at her.

"I've been trying to protect you, but I was wrong." He looked calm, his voice even.

"Don't," I said.

Rhonda's face was wild with fear or madness—it was hard to tell which. "We rid the world of evil. They were *evil.*"

"You're sick," Skip said. "I realize that now. I should never have told you about them. I should have let it drop. What's done is done, but I can't let this go any farther. You need to be stopped." He cocked the gun.

Rhonda cowered, her eyes gleaming, saliva dribbling from her open mouth.

"Wait!" I yelled. I didn't trust myself to grab the gun. The slightest movement and it could go off, and Rhonda would probably catch the bullet. "Don't do it. Maybe you had your reasons for protecting Rhonda. But don't do this. You're not a killer."

Skip stood there a moment, then lowered the gun. "You're right," he said. "I can't. I—"

A brief blast of siren broke the night's stillness. Police cars, which must have approached silently, were suddenly upon us, blue and red lights flashing.

As the door on one car flew open, Skip abruptly brought the gun up, pointed it in his mouth, and pulled the trigger. I averted my eyes just before the blast, feeling sick to my stomach.

Rhonda wailed, a guttural cry like a wounded animal, and threw herself at the body. A burnt gunpowder smell infused the air. I kept my face turned away, listening to Rhonda sobbing and babbling. I felt wet, a little chilly even. I thought I was breaking out in a sweat, until I realized it was raining.

Someone touched my arm. I jumped.

"Hey, hey." It was Duvall. He kept his hand on my arm. "Take it easy."

I released a sigh. "Oh, God."

"When I got your message, I decided to call in reinforcements," he said. "I got in touch with my friend in the department, asked him to have everyone come in silently. I didn't know what we'd find, but I wondered if he might be here." He inclined his head toward Skip's body. "He was Rhonda's half-brother."

Chapter THIRTY-TWO

"The bank," Duvall said. "When you told me about what you found in the office, I got to thinking—what about the cameras? Whoever came in would show up on the bank's cameras.

"It took a while to pinpoint exactly when it happened and who handled the transaction, so we could narrow down which tapes to review. Right away, I recognized him. Himmelfarb is a distinctive name, so it wasn't hard to find a relative—an aunt, up in Towson. She explained the whole thing to me. Rhonda's mother was seeing Skip's father. She got pregnant with Rhonda, but I guess she knew the dad would never leave his family, so she went it alone. The dad kept seeing her, and life went on.

"Skip found out when he followed his dad one day. According to the aunt, their relationship was never the same after that. He shunned his father, not only for having the affair, but for not telling him he had a sister. Skip and Rhonda became friendly. The aunt thinks Skip felt guilty, because he got to live in a nice house with a regular family, while Rhonda and her mom got the short end of the stick."

I nodded. The rain fell harder now. The squad cars' blue and red flashing lights swept across the apartment buildings in a psychedelic clash. A few feet away from me, Skip lay on the ground, half his brain missing, turning cold and white as codfish. Cops had Rhonda by the elbows, leading her from the scene.

Duvall opened an umbrella and stood close enough to shelter us both. "After the accident, Rhonda dropped out of school. The whole thing screwed her up. She had therapy for a while, but her mom couldn't afford to keep that going. Skip's dad tried to help, but he couldn't get too involved—not without blowing things at home.

"Skip finally told his mom about it. That pretty much tore the family apart. He told his aunt he'd never talk to his dad again as long as he lived. Last she heard, Skip was going to get a job and try to help Rhonda out the best he could."

"Sounds like he was trying to be the father Rhonda never had," I said.

"I'd say so."

"I wonder how they ended up at Aces High."

"When I first spoke to Rhonda, she let it slip that she'd heard about the job from an employee," Duvall said. "Skip must have been working there. When he saw Schaeffer and Knudsen and realized who they were, he probably told Rhonda. Skip was always keeping his eyes and ears open, so he might have overheard them talking about the scam they were pulling and seen an opportunity to take revenge."

"Or maybe Rhonda came up with the plan," I said. "Either way, I don't think murder was supposed to be part of it. But from what Rhonda told me, once she pulled the trigger on Knudsen, I think she was ready to do it again to Schaeffer."

Duvall shook his head. "I guess Skip felt so guilty, he was willing to protect Rhonda at his own risk. Maybe he saw those guys as being like his dad—screwing Rhonda over and getting away with it."

"It must have been awful for him," I said. "Wanting to protect Rhonda, but not wanting to be party to murder." I shivered.

"You know," Duvall said, the beginning of a wry smile turning up the corner of his mouth. "You look like you could use a drink."

I smiled. "How 'bout a nice, hot cup of coffee?"

Duvall nodded. "If that's the drink you want, that's what you get." He put a hand on my arm. "Let's go. I've got more to tell you. About Tom Garvey."

ϕ ϕ ϕ

Ray came by after work the next day. He even called first.

"Dinner's on me," he said. "It's the least I can do. And you deserve to celebrate, now that they're dropping the charges against your client."

I knew that wasn't the only reason we were doing this, but I said, "Damn straight. You owe me, Mardovich."

So we had dinner together, like other nights—except I knew it was our last. At least, our last as lovers.

He took me back to my place.

I invited him in and we sat on the sofa together, holding hands. I knew what I had to do, but the words wouldn't come at first. Finally, I opened my mouth and forced myself to say it. "I … I can't do this anymore, you know that."

He nodded. He kept running his thumb over the fingers of one of my hands, studying them, as if for a test.

"I guess it hasn't been easy for you."

"It hurts. When you have to be with them, it hurts. When I couldn't reach you, that hurt, too. I thought I could handle it. I knew it was just for fun." I paused. I could feel my eyes getting wet and blinked to keep the tears at bay. When I trusted myself to speak again, I said, "But it can't be anything … more. We'll never … be able to celebrate our birthdays together or take trips together or …"

I had to stop again. While I was gathering my wits, he said, "I know. I think of you. I know you must get lonely. I feel bad about that."

"And it's not your fault you can't be with me," I said. "You have a wife and kids." I thought about Skip and his father and how disappointed Skip's mother must have been when she found out. His cheating on her all those years, having a child by another mother—it must have felt like her world had fallen apart.

"So, there's more than just us to think about," I continued. "And you love Helen, right?"

He didn't say anything. He continued to stroke my fingers with his thumb.

I heaved a sigh. "So …"

He nodded. Finally, he looked at me. His face was a mask, but his eyes were sad.

"I should go."

"OK."

I didn't draw back when he moved in to kiss me for the last time. When we finally pulled apart, he ran his fingers through my hair. Through some tacit understanding, we rose in unison, hand-in-hand, and walked to the door, our hands linked.

Outside, he paused. "I'll be seeing you," he said.

I managed a smile. "See ya."

Our hands slid apart as he walked away. I returned to the sofa, sat in the same place, and stared at the empty spot where he'd been. I must have done that for ten minutes before I allowed myself to cry.

φ φ φ

Melanie, Donna, and I celebrated a few days later. Donna insisted on paying. We went to a French restaurant and ordered champagne. I tried escargot for the first time. And frog legs. They really do taste like chicken.

After dinner, we considered whether to have cherries jubilee for dessert or another bottle of champagne.

"Whoo!" Melanie flapped a hand in front of her flushed face. "I'm feeling that first bottle still. But what the heck, if you guys want more—" She fell back in her seat and giggled like a kid.

"Well," I said. "After-dinner coffee might be preferable."

"Oh, listen to you," Donna said, her eyes bright. "Such a responsible adult. How about cognac and coffee? Or Irish coffee?"

"You think they serve Irish coffee in a French restaurant?" Melanie's face scrunched into a mock-thoughtful expression.

"I've never had cognac," I said.

Donna's eyes widened. "Cognac it is."

"And coffee," I said. "If it's OK with the guest of honor?"

I looked at Melanie. She grinned back. It was the first time I'd seen her look really happy.

"Whatever you guys want is OK with me," Donna said. "I'm just glad the bank is settling, and we can forget about all this."

"And I'm glad I have my job and my life back." Melanie sighed. "I have one more year to go at Maryland, and I can move on and do something."

I had something to celebrate, too. My credit report had come out clean. I guess Tom died before he had a chance to fully exploit my personal info.

Melanie looked at Donna. "I've made so many mistakes. And you've been good enough to help me out. I won't let you down again."

Donna shook her head. "You didn't let me down."

"Well, before we do anything else," Melanie said, standing up with a slight wobble. "I'm going to find the ladies room. Excuse me."

Donna watched as she ambled off. "I'm so glad it worked out," she said. She looked at me and added, "Thanks, Sam. Thanks for everything."

"Donna, there's something I'm curious about."

"What's that?"

I paused. "Back when Melanie was arrested, I was told that she had a record for shoplifting. I wondered how she could get a job with a bank?"

"I helped her, but she deserved a break. I knew she could be trusted, so I approved the hire."

"Do you do background checks on all the hires?"

"Sure."

"When you did a background check on Tom Garvey, what did you find?"

"The usual things." She began smoothing the unwrinkled tablecloth. "What do you mean?"

"Was there anything peculiar?"

She shrugged. "Uh … no. I mean, he didn't have a record and that's mainly—"

"Did you notice he was seventy-six years old?"

Donna stopped working the cloth. Her shoulders slumped. Slowly, her gaze drifted up to meet mine.

"A private investigator, working in that civil case against Melanie," I said, answering her unstated question. "He found out Knudsen got the information he needed to assume Tom Garvey's identity from his death record. Maybe he was in a rush or maybe he just didn't think about using someone closer to his age."

Donna leaned back and watched a bus boy clean a nearby table. She looked like she'd rather be doing that. "I have no excuses. I could tell you I was busy, that there was pressure on me to bring our system up to speed. It doesn't matter. I should have been more careful, but I didn't even look at his age. Such a simple thing, and I overlooked it."

"You approved his hiring?"

She nodded, a lifeless, puppet-like movement. "God." She squeezed her eyes shut. "If I had *only* been more careful, the whole thing wouldn't have happened. He wouldn't have gotten into our system, he wouldn't have met Melanie, and she'd never have gone through all this." Her voice cracked on the last words.

"That's why you wanted to pay for Melanie's representation," I said. "You felt responsible."

"I've always cared about Melanie. More so since she and her parents … I didn't realize my mistake until after the bank was sued. When I went back and checked more thoroughly, I couldn't believe what I'd done."

Donna put her hand on my wrist. "Please, just don't tell her, Sam. Don't tell her how I was the one who screwed up. It's bad enough I could have lost my job, but ... I don't want to lose her." Her eyes were bright with tears. "She's like a daughter to me."

I patted her hand. "Your secret is safe with me."

Duvall had also said he wouldn't say anything. Leave well enough alone, I thought. Knudsen and Schaeffer were dead, their killer caught. I had served my client well and, in its own way, justice had been done. Leave well enough alone.

Melanie came back, still swaying a bit. "Uhh," she said, plopping into her chair. "You know, guys, maybe we should get dessert and coffee. That champagne ... hey, Donna, what's wrong?"

Donna, who was wiping her eyes, smiled at Melanie. "Nothing at all. I was just telling Sam how *happy* I am that it's over. I'm so happy for you."

Melanie touched Donna's arm. "That's sweet. Thanks." To me, she said, "And thanks to you—again."

I inclined my head. "You're welcome."

We ordered dessert.

Acknowledgments

I would like to thank Pat Altner, Jack Bludis, Carla Buckley, Carolyn Males, Ellen Rawlings, Louise Titchener, and other writers and friends who provided helpful suggestions and encouragement along the way. My thanks to Rennie Hiltz for providing details on medical treatment for internal bleeding. My thanks also to Brian McKenna for providing so many details about strip clubs—stuff I never would have known just by walking into one—and doing such a wonderful job on the original cover art. I'd like to thank Stewart Williams for creating the latest version of the cover. Any errors or omissions on these subjects are my own. And extra special thanks go to Marcia Talley and my other good friends in the Chesapeake Chapter of Sisters in Crime, as well as to publications specialist Laurie Cullen, without whose help I might never have gotten this edition published.

Finally, while this story takes place in real geographic areas and some settings are real, most of them are fictionalized. Any resemblance between a fictionalized place and a similar real one is completely accidental.

Special Acknowledgments

No one gets anywhere in life without help from others. I've always felt lucky to have such a wonderful husband, family, and friends. I'm starting to think that, rather than just being lucky, we choose wisely, and that makes all the difference.

When first I decided to self-publish this book, I never intended to make a living as a self-published author. Things have changed, and now it's possible for almost anyone to do so. However, if you intend to write quality books and establish a real readership, this requires taking the time and effort to produce and market one's books, as well as establish oneself as an author.

I'd like to thank the following people for having faith in me and providing the financial support needed to publish this edition of the book: Ned Adams, Mac Cassity, Debra Hoover-McDonald, Rick Iacangelo on behalf of Mary Louise Iacangelo, Jeanette Lombardi, Nancy Mack for herself and on behalf of Joyce Mack, Karen McQuestion, Julie Simpson, and Kris van der Sande.

I'd like to add very special acknowledgments for Paul Downie and Trevor Veail. To actually find readers in another country and meet them has been a highlight of my writing career.

About the author

Debbi Mack has published three other novels in the Sam McRae mystery series: *Least Wanted*, *Riptide* and *Deep Six*. She's also published a young adult novel, *Invisible Me*, and a thriller, *The Planck Factor*. Debbi has also had several short stories published in various anthologies and been nominated for a Derringer Award.

A former attorney, Debbi has also worked as a journalist, reference librarian, and freelance writer/researcher. She's currently working on a new series of novellas, the first of which has the working title *Damaged Goods*. Along with writing crime fiction, Debbi is branching out into screenplay writing, writing in other genres, and contemplating other projects. Her website is debbimack.com.

CPSIA information can be obtained
at www.ICGtesting.com
Printed in the USA
BVOW11s0847300418
514822BV00002B/378/P